YANKO
THE MVSICIAN
AND OTHER STORIES

HENRYK SIENKIEWICZ

YANKO·THE
MVSICIAN
AND·OTHER
STORIES· 𝄢 𝄢 𝄢 𝄢

BY·HENRYK·SIENKIEWICZ
AVTHOR·OF"·WITH·FIRE
AND·SWORD"·ETC~TRANS
LATED·FROM·THE·POLISH·BY
JEREMIAH·CVRTIN
WITH·DRAWINGS·BY
EDMVND·H·CARRETT

Fredonia Books
Amsterdam, The Netherlands

Yanko the Musician and Other Stories

by
Henryk Sienkiewicz

Translated by Jeremiah Curtin

ISBN: 1-4101-0307-2

Reprinted from the 1893 edition

Fredonia Books
Amsterdam, The Netherlands
http://www.fredoniabooks.com

In order to make original editions of historical works available to scholars at an economical price, this facsimile of the original edition of 1893 is reproduced from the best available copy and has been digitally enhanced to improve legibility, but the text remains unaltered to retain historical authenticity.

PREFACE.

OF the five stories in the present volume, three are of such character that remarks concerning them are not needed, — at least they are not needed here. Readers will prefer to be left to themselves, I think, and might resent comments on Yanko, or Mihas, or the old lighthouse keeper, unless indeed comments coming from other readers whom they meet in social intercourse, or whose impressions are given to the world through the public press.

In two of the stories, however, there are characters not familiar to Americans.

and to these I beg to call attention in this place.

The first of these is the schoolmaster; the other is the officer or general, the man who directs the physical force of the country. The German schoolmaster among the Poles takes the place of the missionary of old times. In past centuries, the reason put forward by Germans for invading Slav lands was, that the people were pagans, that it was necessary to convert them and save their souls. As the conversion was made not by missionaries alone, who worked for the love of God simply, and received their pay in eternal salvation, but by force of arms and the wiles of diplomacy, the missionary was an assistant called in to make the conquest permanent by assimilating the Slavs to the Germans in religion.

This progress of Christianizing was slow, exceedingly bloody and painful, but thorough; and when it was finished the Slavs were exterminated in part, in part converted into the substratum of North German society, excepting only those of them, mainly princes and chiefs, who had succeeded in becoming associated with the conquerors. This historical process took place in the lands between Poznan and the Elbe. In Poznan (Posen) itself modern agencies are in use, because the problem has been modified by time; civilization is the watchword now, not religion. Hence Sienkiewicz presents to us the teachers who brought little Mihas to his death and Bartek the Victor to prison and financial ruin. In Steinmetz we have the higher intelligence with its wiles,— the general who gives the simple-minded Poles at Gravelotte their own music. and

who in leading them against Austria urges
them to conquer the *Niemtsi* (Germans),
he being the quintessence of the German
principle himself. The officers with gold-
rimmed glasses, and the Landrath (p. 267),
give a vivid idea of the realities which
meet a Polish peasant, and of the tragedy
of a people who accomplish the will of
their enemy to the harm of their own
flesh and blood.

                    JEREMIAH CURTIN.

VALENTIA ISLAND, IRELAND,
        August, 1893.

Contents

YANKO
THE MVSICIAN

YANKO THE MUSICIAN.

IT came into the world frail, weak. The gossips, who had gathered around the plank bed of the sick woman, shook their heads over mother and child. The wife of Simon the blacksmith, who was the wisest among them, began to console the sick woman.

"Let me," said she, "light a blessed candle above you. Nothing will come of you,

my gossip; you must prepare for the other
world, and send for the priest to absolve you
from your sins."

"Yes!" said another, "but the boy must
be christened this minute: he cannot wait
for the priest. It is well even to stop him
from becoming a vampire."

So saying, she lighted the blessed candle,
and taking the child sprinkled him with
water till his eyes began to blink; and then
she said: —

"I baptize thee in the name of the Father,
Son, and Holy Ghost. I give thee Yan as
name; and now, Christian soul, go to the
place whence thou camest. Amen!"

But the Christian soul had no wish whatever to go to the place whence it came and
leave its lean little body. It began to kick
with the legs of that body as far as it was
able, and to cry, though so weakly and pitifully
that, as the gossips said, "One would think 't is
a kitten; 't is not a kitten. — what is it?"

They sent for the priest: he came, he did his duty, he went his way, — the sick woman grew better. In a week she went out to her work. The little boy barely "puled," — still, he puled on till in the fourth year the cuckoo brought him sickness in spring; still, he recovered, and with some kind of health reached the tenth year of his life.

He was always lean and sunburnt, with bloated stomach and sunken cheeks; he had a forelock of hemp color almost white and falling on clear staring eyes, looking at the world as if gazing into some immense distance. In winter he used to sit behind the stove and cry in silence from cold, and from hunger too, at times when his mother had nothing to put into the stove or the pot. In the summer he went around in a shirt, with a strip of cloth for a belt, and a straw hat, from beneath the torn brim of which he looked with head peering upward like a bird. His mother, a poor lodger, living from day to

day, like a sparrow under a stranger's roof,
loved him perhaps in her own way; but she
flogged him often enough and called him
"giddy-head" generally.   In the eighth year
of his life he went to herd cattle, or, when
there was nothing to eat in the cottage, to
the pine woods for mushrooms.   It was through
the compassion of God that a wolf did not
eat him.

He was a very dull little fellow, and, like
village children, when spoken to put his
finger in his mouth.   People did not even
promise that he would grow up, and still less
that his mother could expect any good from
him, for he was a poor hand at work.   It is
unknown whence such a creature could have
come; but he was cager for one thing, that
is, music.   He listened to it everywhere, and
when he had grown up a little he thought of
nothing else.   He would go to the woods for
the cattle, or for berries, but would come
home without berries and say stammering, —

"Mamma, something was playing in the woods. Oi! oi!"

And the mother would say: "I'll play for thee, never fear!"

And in fact she made music for him, sometimes with the poker. The boy screamed and promised that he would not do it again, and still he was thinking, "Something is playing out there in the woods." What was it, — did he know? Pines, beeches, golden orioles, all were playing, — the whole forest was playing, and that was the end of it!

The echo, too! In the field the artemisia played for him; in the garden near, the sparrows twittered till the cherry-trees were trembling. In the evening he heard all the voices that were in the village, and thought to himself that certainly the whole village was playing. When they sent him to work to spread manure, even then the wind played on the fork-tines.

The overseer caught him once standing

with dishevelled forelock and listening to the wind on the wooden tines: he looked at the boy, and unbuckling his leather belt, gave him a good keepsake. But what use in that? The people called him " Yanko the musician." In the springtime he ran away from the house to make whistles near the river. In the night, when the frogs were croaking, the land-rail calling in the meadows, the bittern screaming in the dew, the cocks crowing behind the wicker fences, he could not sleep, — he did nothing but listen; and God alone knows what he heard in that playing. His mother could not take him to church, for as soon as the organ began to roar or the choir sang in sweet voices, the child's eyes were covered with mist, and were as if not looking out of this world.

The watchman who walked through the village at night and counted the stars in the sky to keep from sleeping, or conversed in a low voice with the dogs, saw more than once the white shirt of Yanko stealing along in the darkness toward the public house. But the boy was not going to the public house, only near it. There he would cower at the wall and listen. The people were dancing the *obertas;* at times some young fellow would cry, "U-ha!" The stamping of boots was heard; then the querying voices of girls, "What?" The fiddles sang in low tones: "We will eat, we will drink, we shall be merry;" and the bass viol accompanied in a deep voice, with importance: "As God gave! As God gave!" The windows were gleaming with life, and every beam in the house seemed to tremble, singing and playing also; but Yanko was listening.

How much would he give to have such a fiddle playing thinly: "We will eat, we will drink, we shall be merry"! Such singing bits of wood! But from what place could he get them, — where were they made? If they would just let him hold such a thing in his hand

even once! How could that be? He was
only free to listen, and then to listen only
till the voice of the watchman was heard
behind him in the darkness, —

"Wilt thou go home, little devil?"

Then he fled away home in his bare feet,
but in the darkness behind him ran the voice
of the fiddle: "We will eat, we will drink,
we shall be merry," and the deep voice of
the bass: "As God gave! As God gave! As
God gave!"

Whenever he could hear a fiddle at a harvest-
home or some wedding, it was a great holiday
for him. After that he went behind the stove
and said nothing for whole days, looking
like a cat in the dark with gleaming eyes.
Then he made himself a fiddle out of a shingle
and some horsehair, but it would not play
beautifully like that one in the public house, — it
sounded low, very low, just like mice of some
kind, or gnats. He played on it however from
morning till evening; though for doing that he

got so many cuffs that at last he looked like a pinched, unripe apple. But such was his nature. The poor child became thinner and thinner, only he had always a big stomach; his forelock grew thicker and thicker, and his eyes opened more and more widely, though filled oftener with tears; but his cheeks and his breast fell in more and more.

He was not at all like other children; he was rather like his fiddle formed of a shingle, which hardly made a noise. Before harvest, besides, he was suffering from hunger, for he lived most frequently on raw carrots, and also the wish to possess a fiddle. But that wish did not turn out well for him.

At the mansion the lackey had a fiddle and he played on it sometimes at twilight to please the waiting-maid. Yanko crept up at times among the burdocks as far as the open door of the pantry to look at it. It hung on the wall opposite the door; the boy would send his whole soul out to it through his eyes, for

2

it seemed to him that that was some unattainable object, which he was unworthy to touch, that that was some kind of dearest love of his. Still he wanted it. He would like to have it in his hand at least one time, to look at it near by. The poor little fellow's heart trembled from happiness at the thought.

A certain night there was no one in the pantry. Their lordships had been in foreign countries for some time, the house was empty, the lackey was at the other side with the waiting-maid. Yanko, lurking in the burdocks, had been looking for a long time through the broad door at the object of all his desires. The moon in the sky was full, and shone in with sloping rays through the pantry window, which it reflected in the form of a great quadrangle on the opposite wall. The quadrangle approached the fiddle gradually and at last illuminated every bit of it. At that time it seemed in the dark depth as if a silver light shone from the fiddle, — especially

the plump bends in it were lighted so strongly
that Yanko could barely look at them. In
that light everything was perfectly visible, — the
sides with incisions, the strings, and the bent
handle. The pegs in it gleamed like fireflies,
and at its side was hung the bow in the form
of a silver rod.

Ah, all was beautiful and almost enchanted;
and Yanko looked more and more greedily.
He was crouched in the burdocks, with his
elbows pressed on his lean knees; with open
eyes he looked and looked. Now terror held
him to the spot, now a certain unconquerable
desire pushed him forward. Was that some
enchantment, or what? But the fiddle in the
bright light seemed sometimes to approach,
as it were to float toward the boy. At times
it grew darker, to shine up again still more.
Enchantment, clearly enchantment! Then the
breeze blew; the trees rustled quietly, there
was a noise in the burdocks, and Yanko heard,
as it were, distinctly, —

"Go, Yanko, there is no one in the pantry; go, Yanko!"

The night was clear, bright. In the garden a nightingale began to sing and whistled with a low voice, then louder. "Go! go in! take it." An honest wood-owl turned in flight around the child's head, and cried: "Yanko, no! no!" The owl flew away, but the nightingale and the burdocks muttered more distinctly: "There is no one inside!" The fiddle shone again.

The poor little bent figure pushed forward slowly and carefully; meanwhile the nightingale was whistling in a very low voice, "Go! go in! take it!"

The white shirt appeared nearer and nearer to the pantry. The dark burdocks covered it no longer. On the threshold of the pantry was to be heard quick breathing from the weak breast of the child. A moment more the white shirt has vanished; there is only one naked foot outside the threshold. In vain.

O wood-owl, dost thou fly once again and cry: "No! no!" Yanko is in the pantry.

The great frogs began to croak in the garden pond, as if frightened, but afterward grew silent. The nightingale ceased to sing, the burdocks to rustle. Meanwhile Yanko crept along silently and carefully, but all at once fear seized him. In the burdocks he felt as if at home, as a wild beast feels in the thicket; but now he was like a wild beast in a trap. His movements became hurried, his breath short and whistling; at the same time, darkness seized hold of him. A quiet summer lightning flashed between the east and west, and lighted up once more the interior of the pantry, and Yanko on all fours with his head turned upward. But the lightning was quenched, a small cloud hid the moon, and nothing was to be seen or heard.

After a while a sound came out from the darkness, very low and complaining, as if some one had touched strings unguardedly, and on a sudden some rough, drowsy voice, coming out of the corner of the pantry, asked angrily, —

"Who is there?"

Yanko held his breath in his breast, but the rude voice inquires again, —

"Who is there?"

A match became visible on the wall; there was a light, and then — Oh, my God! curses, blows, the wailing of a child, and crying "Oh, for God's sake!" — the barking of dogs, moving of lights behind the window, a noise through the whole building!

The next day Yanko stood before the tribunal of the village mayor.

Was he to be tried as a criminal? Of course! The mayor and elders looked at him as he stood before them with his finger in his mouth, with staring and terrified eyes, small, poor, starved, beaten, not knowing where he was or what they wanted of him. How judge such a poor little misery, who was ten years of age, and barely able to stand on his legs? Send him to prison, — how help it? Still it was necessary to have some small mercy on children. Let the watchman take him and give him a flogging, so that he won't steal a second time, and that's the whole business.

It was indeed !

They called Stah, who was the night watch.

"Take him and give him something for a keepsake."

Stah nodded his dull beastlike head, thrust Yanko under his arm as he would a cat, and took him out to the barn. The child, whether he failed to understand what the question was, or whether he was frightened — 't is enough that he uttered not a syllable; he merely stared like a bird. Did he know what they were doing with him? Only when Stah took the handful to the stable, stretched it on the ground, and raising the shirt from it struck a full blow, only then did Yanko scream, " Mother ! " and

as long as Stah flogged him he cried, "Mother!
mother!" but always lower and weaker, until
after a certain blow the child called mother
no longer.

The poor broken fiddle!

Ai, stupid, angry Stah, who beats children
that way? Besides, this one is small and
weak, hardly living.

The mother came, took the little boy, but
had to carry him home. The next day Yanko
did not rise from the bed, and the third day,
in the evening, he died quietly on the plank
cot under hemp matting.

The swallows were twittering in the cherry-
tree which grew at the cottage; the rays of
the sun entered through the window pane
and colored with the brightness of gold the
dishevelled hair of the little boy and the face
in which there remained not a drop of blood.
That ray was as it were a road upon which
the soul of the boy was to go away. It
was well that it went out by a broad shining

road in the moment of death, for during life it went on a thorny one, truly. Meanwhile the emaciated breast moved with another breath, and the face of the child was as if absorbed in listening to the sounds of the village which came in through the open window. It was evening, so the girls coming back from hay-making were singing, "Oi, on the green field!" and from the stream came the playing of pipes. Yanko listened for the last time to the sounds of the village. On the matting lay the shingle fiddle at his side.

All at once the face of the dying boy lighted up, and from his whitening lips came out the whisper, "Mother!"

"What, my son?" answered the mother, whom tears were choking.

"Mother, will the Lord God give me a real fiddle in heaven?"

"He will, my son, He will give thee one," answered the mother; but she could speak no longer, for suddenly in her hard breast burst the gathering sorrow, and groaning only, "O Jesus! O Jesus!" she fell with her face on a box, and began to wail as if she had lost her reason, or as a man wails who sees that he cannot wrest from death the beloved one.

In fact, she did not wrest him; for when she raised herself again she looked at the child. The eyes of the little musician were open, it is true, but fixed; his face was very dignified, gloomy, and rigid. The ray of the sun had gone also.

Peace to thee, Yanko.

.   .   .   .

On the second day the master and mistress of the mansion returned to their residence from Italy, with their daughter and the cavalier who was paying court to her. The cavalier said, —

"Quel beau pay que l'Italie!"

"And what a people of artists! On est heureux de chercher là-bas des talents et de les protéger," added the young lady.

The birches were murmuring above Yanko.

THE
LIGHT-HOVSE
KEEPER OF ASPINWALL

THE LIGHT-HOUSE KEEPER OF ASPINWALL

CHAPTER·I

ON a time it happened that the light-house keeper in Aspinwall, not far from Panama, disappeared without a trace. Since he disappeared during a storm, it was supposed that the ill-fated man went to the very edge of the small, rocky island on which the light-house stood, and was swept out by a wave. This supposition seemed the more likely as his boat was not found next day in its rocky niche. The place of light-house keeper had become vacant. It was necessary to fill this place at the earliest moment possible, since the light-house had no small significance for the local movement as well as for vessels going from New York to Panama. Mosquito Bay abounds in sandbars and banks. Among these navigation even in the daytime is difficult; but at night, especially with the fogs which are so frequent on those waters warmed by the sun of the tropics, it is nearly impossible. The only guide at that time for the numerous vessels is the light-house.

The task of finding a new keeper fell to the United States consul living in Panama, and this task was no small one : first, because it was absolutely necessary to find the man within twelve hours; second, the man must be unusually conscientious, — it was not possible, of course, to take the first comer at random; finally, there was an utter lack of candidates. Life on a tower is uncommonly difficult, and by no means enticing to people of the South, who love idleness and the freedom of a vagrant life. That light-house keeper is almost a prisoner. He cannot leave his rocky island except on Sundays. A boat from Aspinwall brings him provisions and water once a day, and returns immediately; on the whole island, one acre in area, there is no inhabitant. The keeper lives in the light-house; he keeps it in order. During the day he gives signals by displaying flags of various colors to indicate changes of the barometer; in the evening he lights the lantern. This would be no great labor were it not that to reach the lantern at the summit of the tower he must pass over more than four hundred steep and very high steps; sometimes he must make this journey repeatedly during the day. In general it is the life of a monk, and indeed more than that, — the life of a hermit. It was not wonderful, therefore, that Mr. Isaac Falconbridge was in no small anxiety as to where he should find a permanent successor to the recent keeper; and it is easy to understand his joy when a successor announced himself most unexpectedly on that very day. He was a man already old, seventy years or more, but fresh, erect, with the movements and bearing of a soldier. His hair was perfectly white, his face as dark as that of a Creole; but judging from his blue eyes, he did not belong to a people of the South. His face was somewhat downcast and sad, but honest. At the first glance he pleased Falconbridge. It remained only to examine him. Therefore the following conversation began: —

"Where are you from?"

"I am a Pole."

"Where have you worked up to this time?"

"In one place and another."

"A light-house keeper should like to stay in one place."

"I need rest."

"Have you served? Have you testimonials of honorable government service?"

The old man drew from his bosom a piece of faded silk resembling a strip of an old flag, unwound it, and said : —

"Here are the testimonials. I received this cross in 1830. This second one is Spanish, from the Carlist War; the third is the French legion; the fourth I received in Hungary. Afterward I fought in the States against the South; there they do not give crosses."

Falconbridge took the paper and began to read.

"H'm! Skavinski? Is that your name? H'm! Two flags captured in a bayonet attack. You were a gallant soldier."

"I am able to be a conscientious light-house keeper."

"It is necessary to ascend the tower a number of times daily. Have you sound legs?"

"I crossed the plains on foot." (The immense steppes between the East and California are called "the plains.")

"Do you know sea service?"

"I served three years on a whaler."

"You have tried various occupations."

"The only one I have not known is quiet."

"Why is that?"

The old man shrugged his shoulders. "Such is my fate."

"Still you seem to me too old for a light-house keeper."

"Sir," exclaimed the candidate suddenly, in a voice of emotion, "I am greatly wearied, knocked about. I have passed through much, as you see. This place is one of those which I have wished for most ardently. I am old, I need rest. I need to say to myself, 'Here you will remain; this is your port.' Ah, sir, this depends now on you alone. Another time perhaps such a place will not offer itself. What luck that I was in Panama! I entreat you — as God is dear to me, I am like a ship which if it misses the harbor will be lost. If you wish to make an old man happy — I swear to you that I am honest, but — I have enough of wandering."

The blue eyes of the old man expressed such earnest entreaty that Falconbridge, who had a good, simple heart, was touched.

"Well," said he, "I take you. You are light-house keeper."

The old man's face gleamed with inexpressible joy.

"I thank you."

"Can you go to the tower to-day?"

"I can."

"Then good-by. Another word, for any failure in service you will be dismissed."

"All right."

That same evening, when the sun had descended on the other side of the isthmus, and a day of sunshine was followed by a night without twilight, the new keeper was in his place evidently, for the light-house was casting its bright rays on the water as usual. The night was perfectly calm, silent, genuinely tropical, filled with a transparent haze, forming around the moon a great colored rainbow with soft,

unbroken edges; the sea was moving only
because the tide raised it. Skavinski on the
balcony seemed from below like a small black
point. He tried to collect his thoughts, and
take in his new position; but his mind was too
much under pressure to move with regularity.
He felt somewhat as a hunted beast feels when
at last it has found refuge from pursuit on some
inaccessible rock or in a cave. There had
come to him finally an hour of quiet; the
feeling of safety filled his soul with a certain
unspeakable bliss. Now on that rock he can
simply laugh at his previous wanderings, his
misfortunes and failures. He was in truth like
a ship whose masts, ropes, and sails had been
broken and rent by a tempest, and cast from
the clouds to the bottom of the sea, — a ship
on which the tempest had hurled waves and
spat foam, but which still wound its way to
the harbor. The pictures of that storm passed
quickly through his mind as he compared it
with the calm future now beginning. A part

of his wonderful adventures he had related to
Falconbridge ; he had not mentioned, however,
thousands of other incidents. It had been his
misfortune that as often as he pitched his tent
and fixed his fireplace to settle down perma-
nently, some wind tore out the stakes of his tent,
whirled away the fire, and bore him on toward
destruction. Looking now from the balcony of
the tower at the illuminated waves, he remembered everything through which he had passed.
He had campaigned in the four parts of the
world, and in wandering had tried almost every
occupation. Labor-loving and honest, more
than once had he earned money, and had
always lost it in spite of every prevision and
the utmost caution. He had been a gold-
miner in Australia, a diamond-digger in Africa,
a rifleman in public service in the East Indies.
He established a ranch in California, — the
drought ruined him ; he tried trading with
wild tribes in the interior of Brazil, — his raft
was wrecked on the Amazon : he himself alone.

weaponless, and nearly naked, wandered in the forest for many weeks, living on wild fruits, exposed every moment to death from the jaws of wild beasts. He established a forge in Helena, Arkansas, and that was burned in a great fire which consumed the whole town. Next he fell into the hands of Indians in the Rocky Mountains, and only through a miracle was he saved by Canadian trappers. Then he served as a sailor on a vessel running between Bahia and Bordeaux, and as harpooner on a whaling-ship; both vessels were wrecked. He had a cigar factory in Havana, and was robbed by his partner while he himself was lying sick with the vomito. At last he came to Aspinwall, and there was to be the end of his failures, — for what could reach him on that rocky island? Neither water nor fire nor men. But from men Skavinski had not suffered much; he had met good men oftener than bad ones.

But it seemed to him that all the four elements were persecuting him. Those who knew him said that he had no luck, and with that they explained everything. He himself became somewhat of a monomaniac. He believed that some mighty and vengeful hand was pursuing him everywhere, on all lands and waters. He did not like, however, to speak of this; only at times, when some one asked him whose hand that could be, he pointed mysteriously to the Polar Star, and said, " It comes from that place." In reality his failures were so continuous that they were wonderful, and might easily drive a nail into the head, especially of the man who had experienced them. But Skavinski had the patience of an Indian, and that great calm power of resistance which comes from truth of heart. In his time he had received in Hungary a number of bayonet-thrusts because he would not grasp at a stirrup which was shown as means of salvation to him, and cry for quarter. In like manner he did not bend to misfortune. He crept up against the mountain as industriously as an ant. Pushed down a hundred times, he began his journey calmly for the hundred and first time. He was in his way a most peculiar original. This old soldier, tempered God knows in how many fires, hardened in suffering, hammered and forged, had the heart of a child. In the time of the epidemic in Cuba, the vomito attacked him because he had given to the sick all his quinine, of which he had a considerable supply, and left not a grain to himself.

There had been in him also this wonderful quality, — that after so many disappointments he was ever full of confidence, and did not lose hope that all would be well yet. In winter he grew lively, and predicted great events. He waited for these events with impatience, and lived with the thought of them whole summers. But the winters passed one after another, and Skavinski lived only to this, — that they whitened his head. At last he grew old, began to lose energy; his endurance was becoming more and more like resignation, his former calmness was tending toward supersensitiveness, and that tempered soldier was degenerating into a man ready to shed tears for any cause. Besides this, from time to time he was weighed down by a terrible homesickness which was roused by any circumstance, — the sight of swallows, gray birds like sparrows, snow on the mountains, or melancholy music like that heard on a time. Finally, there was one idea which mastered him, — the idea of rest. It mastered the old man thoroughly, and swallowed all other desires and hopes. This ceaseless wanderer could not imagine anything more to be longed for, anything more precious, than a quiet corner in which to rest, and wait in silence for the end. Perhaps specially because some whim of fate had so hurried him over all seas and lands that he could hardly catch his breath, did he imagine that the highest human happiness was simply not to wander. It is true that such modest happiness was his

due ; but he was so accustomed to disappointments that he thought of rest as people in
general think of something which is beyond
reach. He did not dare to hope for it. Meanwhile, unexpectedly in the course of twelve
hours he had gained a position which was as if
chosen for him out of all in the world. We
are not to wonder, then, that when he lighted
his lantern in the evening he became as it were
dazed, — that he asked himself if that was
reality, and he did not dare to answer that it
was. But at the same time reality convinced
him with incontrovertible proofs ; hence hours
one after another passed while he was on
the balcony. He gazed, and convinced himself. It might seem that he was looking at
the sea for the first time in his life. The
lens of the lantern cast into the darkness an
enormous triangle of light, beyond which the
eye of the old man was lost in the black distance completely, in the distance mysterious and
awful. But that distance seemed to run toward

the light. The long waves following one another rolled out from the darkness, and went
bellowing toward the base of the island; and
then their foaming backs were visible, shining
rose-colored in the light of the lantern. The
incoming tide swelled more and more, and covered the sandy bars. The mysterious speech
of the ocean came with a fulness more powerful and louder, at one time like the thunder
of cannon, at another like the roar of great
forests, at another like the distant dull sound
of the voices of people. At moments it was
quiet; then to the ears of the old man came
some great sigh, then a kind of sobbing, and
again threatening outbursts. At last the wind
bore away the haze, but brought black, broken
clouds, which hid the moon. From the west
it began to blow more and more; the waves
sprang with rage against the rock of the light-
house, licking with foam the foundation walls.
In the distance a storm was beginning to bellow.
On the dark, disturbed expanse certain green

lanterns gleamed from the masts of ships. These green points rose high and then sank; now they swayed to the right, and now to the left. Skavinski descended to his room. The storm began to howl. Outside people on those ships were struggling with night, with darkness, with waves; but inside the tower it was calm and still. Even the sounds of the storm hardly came through the thick walls, and only the measured tick-tack of the clock lulled the wearied old man to his slumber.

THE
LIGHT-HOUSE
KEEPER of ASPINWALL
CHAPTER·II

HOURS, days, and weeks began to pass. Sailors assert that sometimes when the sea is greatly roused, something from out the midst of night and darkness calls them by name. If the infinity of the sea may call out thus, perhaps when a man is growing old, calls come to him, too, from another infinity still darker and more deeply mysterious; and the more he is wearied by life the dearer are those calls to

him. But to hear them quiet is needed.
Besides, old age loves to put itself aside as if
with a foreboding of the grave. The light-
house had become for Skavinski such a half
grave. Nothing is more monotonous than life
on a beacon-tower. If young people consent
to take up this service they leave it after a
time. Light-house keepers are generally men
not young, gloomy, and confined to themselves.
If by chance one of them leaves his light-house
and goes among men, he walks in the midst of
them like a person roused from deep slumber.
On the tower there is a lack of minute impressions which in ordinary life teach men to adapt
themselves to everything. All that a light-
house keeper comes in contact with is gigantic, and devoid of definitely outlined forms.
The sky is one whole, the water another ; and
between those two infinities the soul of man is
in loneliness. That is a life in which thought is
continual meditation, and out of that meditation
nothing rouses the keeper, not even his work.

Day is like day as two beads in a rosary, unless changes of weather form the only variety. But Skavinski felt more happiness than ever in life before. He rose with the dawn, took his breakfast, polished the lens, and then sitting on the balcony gazed into the distance of the water; and his eyes were never sated with the pictures which he saw before him. On the enormous turquoise ground of the ocean were to be seen generally flocks of swollen sails gleaming in the rays of the sun so brightly that the eyes were blinking before the excess of light. Sometimes the ships, favored by the so-called trade winds, went in an extended line one after another, like a chain of sea-mews or alba-trosses. The red casks indicating the channel swayed on the light wave with gentle move-ment. Among the sails appeared every afternoon gigantic grayish feather-like plumes of smoke. That was a steamer from New York which brought passengers and goods to Aspinwall, drawing behind it a frothy path of foam. On

the other side of the balcony Skavinski saw as
if on his palm Aspinwall and its busy harbor,
and in it a forest of masts, boats, and craft; a
little farther white houses and the towers of the
town.   From the height of his tower the small
houses were like the nests of sea-mews, the
boats were like beetles, and the people moved
around like small points on the white stone
boulevard.   From early morning a light eastern
breeze brought a confused hum of human life,
above which predominated the whistle of
steamers.   In the afternoon six o'clock came;
the movement in the harbor began to cease;
the mews hid themselves in the rents of the
cliffs; the waves grew feeble and became in
some sort lazy; and then on the land, on the
sea, and on the tower came a time of stillness
unbroken by anything.   The yellow sands from
which the waves had fallen back glittered like
golden stripes on the width of the waters; the
body of the tower was outlined definitely in
blue.   Floods of sunbeams were poured from

the sky on the water and the sands and the cliff. At that time a certain lassitude full of sweetness seized the old man. He felt that the rest which he was enjoying was excellent; and when he thought that it would be continuous nothing was lacking to him.

Skavinski was intoxicated with his own happiness; and since a man adapts himself easily to improved conditions, he gained faith and confidence by degrees; for he thought that if men built houses for invalids, why should not God gather up at last his own invalids? Time passed, and confirmed him in this conviction. The old man grew accustomed to his tower, to the lantern, to the rock, to the sand bars, to solitude. He grew accustomed also to the sea-mews which hatched in the crevices of the rock and in the evening held meetings on the roof of the light-house. Skavinski threw to them generally the remnants of his food; and soon they grew tame, and afterward when he fed them a real storm of white wings encircled him, and the old man

went among the birds like a shepherd among
sheep. When the tide ebbed he went to the
low sand-banks, on which he collected savory
periwinkles and beautiful pearl shells of the
nautilus, which receding waves had left on the
sand. In the night by the moonlight and the
tower he went to catch fish, which frequented
the windings of the cliff in myriads. At last
he was in love with his rocks and his treeless
little island, grown over only with small thick
plants exuding sticky resin. The distant views
repaid him for the poverty of the island, however. During afternoon hours, when the air
became very clear he could see the whole isthmus covered with the richest vegetation. It
seemed to Skavinski at such times that he saw
one gigantic garden, — bunches of cocoa, and
enormous musa, combined as it were in luxu-
rious tufted bouquets, right there behind the
houses of Aspinwall. Farther on, between Aspinwall and Panama, was a great forest over which
every morning and evening hung a reddish haze

of exhalations,— a real tropical forest with its feet in stagnant water, interlaced with lianas and filled with the sound of one sea of gigantic orchids, palms, milk-trees, iron-trees, gum-trees.

Through his field-glass the old man could see not only trees and the broad leaves of bananas, but even legions of monkeys and great marabous and flocks of parrots, rising at times like a rainbow cloud over the forest. Skavinski knew such forests well, for after being wrecked on the Amazon he had wandered whole weeks among similar arches and thickets. He had seen how many dangers and deaths lie concealed under those wonderful and smiling exteriors. During the nights which he had spent in them he heard close at hand the sepulchral voices of howling monkeys and the roaring of the jaguars; he saw gigantic serpents coiled like lianas on trees; he knew those slumbering forest lakes full of torpedo-fish and swarming with crocodiles; he knew under what a yoke man lives in those unexplored wildernesses in which are single

leaves that exceed a man's size ten times, —
wildernesses swarming with blood-drinking
mosquitoes, tree-leaches, and gigantic poisonous
spiders. He had experienced that forest life
himself, had witnessed it, had passed through it ;
therefore it gave him the greater enjoyment to
look from his height and gaze on those *matos*,
admire their beauty, and be guarded from their
treacherousness. His tower preserved him
from every evil. He left it only for a few
hours on Sunday. He put on then his blue
keeper's coat with silver buttons, and hung his
crosses on his breast. His milk-white head
was raised with a certain pride when he heard
at the door, while entering the church, the
Creoles say among themselves, " We have an
honorable light-house keeper and not a here-
tic, though he is a Yankee." But he returned
straightway after Mass to his island, and returned
happy, for he had still no faith in the mainland.
On Sunday also he read the Spanish newspaper
which he bought in the town, or the " New York

Herald," which he borrowed from Falconbridge ;
and he sought in it European news eagerly.
The poor old heart on that light-house tower
and in another hemisphere was beating yet for
its birthplace. At times too, when the boat
brought his daily supplies and water to the
island, he went down from the tower to talk
with Johnson, the guard. But after a while he
seemed to grow shy. He ceased to go to the
town to read the papers and to go down to talk
politics with Johnson. Whole weeks passed in
this way, so that no one saw him and he saw no
one. The only signs that the old man was living were the disappearance of the provisions
left on shore, and the light of the lantern
kindled every evening with the same regularity
with which the sun rose in the morning from
the waters of those regions. Evidently the old
man had become indifferent to the world.
Homesickness was not the cause, but just this, —
that even homesickness had passed into resignation. The whole world began now and ended

for Skavinski on his island. He had grown accustomed to the thought that he would not leave the tower till his death, and he simply forgot that there was anything else besides it. Moreover, he had become a mystic; his mild blue eyes began to stare like the eyes of a child, and were as if fixed on something at a distance. In presence of a surrounding uncommonly simple and great, the old man was losing the feeling of personality; he was ceasing to exist as an individual, was becoming merged more and more in that which inclosed him. He did not understand anything beyond his environment; he felt only unconsciously. At last it seems to him that the heavens, the water, his rock, the tower, the golden sand-banks, and the swollen sails, the sea-mews, the ebb and flow of the tide, — all form a mighty unity, one enormous mysterious soul; that he is sinking in that mystery, and feels that soul which lives and lulls itself. He sinks and is rocked.

forgets himself; and in that narrowing of his own individual existence, in that half-waking, half-sleeping, he has discovered a rest so great that it nearly resembles half-death.

THE
LIGHT-HOUSE·KEEPER·OF·
ASPINWALL· CHAPTER·III.

BUT the awakening came.

On a certain day, when the boat brought water and a supply of provisions, Skavinski came down an hour later from the tower, and saw that besides the usual cargo there was an additional package. On the outside of this package were postage stamps of the United States, and the address, "Skavinski, Esq.," written on coarse canvas.

The old man with aroused curiosity cut the canvas, and saw books; he took one in his hand, looked at it, and put it back; thereupon his hands began to tremble greatly. He covered his eyes as if he did not believe them; it seemed to him as if he were dreaming. The book was Polish, — what did that mean? Who could have sent the book? Clearly, it did not occur to him at the first moment that in the beginning of his light-house career he had read in the "Herald," borrowed from the consul, of the formation of a Polish society in New York, and had sent at once to that society half his month's salary, for which he had, more-over, no use on the tower. The society had sent him the books with thanks. The books came in the natural way; but at the first moment the old man could not seize those thoughts. Polish books in Aspinwall, on his tower, amid his solitude, — that was for him something uncommon, a certain breath from past times, a kind of miracle. Now it seemed

to him, as to those sailors in the night, that
something was calling him by name with a
voice greatly beloved and nearly forgotten.   He
sat for a while with closed eyes, and was
almost certain that, when he opened them, the
dream would be gone.

The package, cut open, lay before him, shone
upon clearly by the afternoon sun, and on it
was an open book. When the old man
stretched his hand toward it again, he heard in
the stillness the beating of his own heart.   He
looked; it was poetry. On the outside stood
printed in great letters the title, underneath the
name of the author. The name was not strange
to Skavinski; he saw that it belonged to the
great poet,[1] whose productions he had read in
1830 in Paris. Afterward when campaigning
in Algiers and Spain, he had heard from his
countrymen of the growing fame of the great
seer; but he was so accustomed to the musket

---

[1] Mickiewicz (pronounced Mitskyevich), the greatest
poet of Poland.

at that time that he took no book in hand.
In 1849 he went to America, and in the adven-
turous life which he led, he hardly ever met a
Pole, and never a Polish book.   With the
greater eagerness, therefore, and with a livelier
beating of the heart, did he turn to the title-
page.   It seemed to him then that on his lonely
rock some solemnity is about to take place.
Indeed, it was a moment of great calm and
silence.   The clocks of Aspinwall were striking
five in the afternoon.   Not a cloud darkened
the clear sky ; only a few sea-mews were sailing
through the air.   The ocean was as if cradled
to sleep.   The waves on the shore stammered
quietly, spreading softly on the sand.   In the
distance the white houses of Aspinwall, and the
wonderful groups of palm, were smiling.   In
truth, there was something there solemn, calm,
and full of dignity.   Suddenly in the midst of
that calm of Nature was heard the trembling
voice of the old man, who read aloud as if to
understand himself better. —

"Thou art like health, O my birth-land Litva ![1]
    How much we should prize thee he only can know who
        has lost thee.
    Thy beauty in perfect adornment this day
    I see and describe, because I am yearning for thee."

His voice failed Skavinski. The letters began
to dance before his eyes; something broke
in his breast, and went like a wave from his
heart higher and higher, choking his voice and
pressing his throat. A moment more he con-
trolled himself, and read further, —

"O Holy Lady, who guardest bright Chenstohova,
    Who shinest in Ostrobrama and preservest
    The castle town Novgrodek with its trusty people,
    As Thou didst give me back to health in childhood,
    When by my weeping mother placed beneath Thy
        care
    I raised my lifeless eyelids upward,
    And straightway walked unto Thy holy threshold,
    To thank God for the life restored me, —
    So by a wonder now restore us to the bosom of our
        birthplace."

                    [1] Lithuania.

The swollen wave broke through the restraint of his will. The old man sobbed, and threw himself on the ground; his milk-white hair was mingled with the sand of the sea. Forty years had passed since he had seen his country, and God knows how many since he heard his native speech; and now that speech had come to him itself, — it had sailed to him over the ocean, and found him in solitude on another hemisphere, — it so loved, so dear, so beautiful ! In the sobbing which shook him there was no pain, — only a suddenly aroused immense love, in the presence of which other things are as nothing. With that great weeping he had simply implored forgiveness of that beloved one, set aside because he had grown so old, had become so accustomed to his solitary rock, and had so forgotten it that in him even longing had begun to disappear. But now it returned as if by a miracle; therefore the heart leaped in him.

Moments vanished one after another; he lay

there continually. The mews flew over the light-house, crying as if alarmed for their old friend. The hour in which he fed them with the remnants of his food had come; therefore, some of them flew down from the light-house to him; then more and more came, and began to pick and to shake their wings over his head. The sound of the wings roused him. He had wept his fill, and had now a certain calm and brightness; but his eyes were as if inspired. He gave unwittingly all his provisions to the birds, which rushed at him with an uproar, and he himself took the book again. The sun had gone already behind the gardens and the forest of Panama, and was going slowly beyond the isthmus to the other ocean; but the Atlantic was full of light yet; in the open air there was still perfect vision; therefore, he read further: —

"Now bear my longing soul to those forest slopes, to
    those green meadows."

At last the dusk obliterates the letters on the white paper, — the dusk short as a twinkle. The old man rested his head on the rock, and closed his eyes. Then "She who defends bright Chenstohova" took his soul, and transported it to "those fields colored by various grain." On the sky were burning yet those long stripes, red and golden, and on those brightnesses he was flying to beloved regions. The pine-woods were sounding in his ears; the streams of his native place were murmuring. He saw everything as it was; everything asked him, "Dost remember?" He remembers! he sees broad fields, between the fields, woods and villages. It is night now. At this hour his lantern usually illuminates the darkness of the sea; but now he is in his native village. His old head has dropped on his breast, and he is dreaming. Pictures are passing before his eyes quickly, and a little disorderly. He does not see the house in which he was born, for war had destroyed it; he does not

5

see his father and mother, for they died when
he was a child; but still the village is as if
he had left it yesterday, — the line of cottages
with lights in the windows, the mound, the
mill, the two ponds opposite each other, and
thundering all night with a chorus of frogs.
Once he had been on guard in that village all
night; now that past stood before him at once
in a series of views. He is an Ulan again, and
he stands there on guard; at a distance is the
public house; he looks with swimming eyes.
There is thundering and singing and shouting
amid the silence of the night with voices of
fiddles and bass-viols "U-ha! U-ha!" Then
the Ulans knock out fire with their horseshoes,
and it is wearisome for him there on his horse.
The hours drag on slowly; at last the lights
are quenched; now as far as the eye reaches
there is mist, and mist impenetrable; now the
fog rises, evidently from the fields, and embraces the whole world with a whitish cloud.
You would say, a complete ocean. But that

is fields; soon the land-rail will be heard in the darkness, and the bitterns will call from the reeds. The night is calm and cool, in truth a Polish night! In the distance the pine-wood is sounding without wind, like the roll of the sea. Soon dawn will whiten the East. In fact, the cocks are beginning to crow behind the hedges. One answers to another from cottage to cottage; the storks are screaming somewhere on high. The Ulan feels well and bright. Someone had spoken of a battle to-morrow. Hei! that will go on, like all the others, with shouting, with fluttering of flag-lets. The young blood is playing like a trumpet, though the night cools it. But it is dawning. Already night is growing pale; out of the shadows come forests, the thicket, a row of cottages, the mill, the poplars. The well is squeaking like a metal banner on a tower. What a beloved land, beautiful in the rosy gleams of the morning! Oh, the one land, the one land!

Quiet! the watchful picket hears that some one is approaching. Of course, they are coming to relieve the guard.

Suddenly some voice is heard above Skavinski. —

"Here, old man! Get up! What's the matter?"

The old man opens his eyes, and looks with wonder at the person standing before him. The remnants of the dream-visions struggle in his head with reality. At last the visions pale and vanish. Before him stands Johnson, the harbor guide.

"What's this?" asked Johnson; "are you sick?"

"No."

"You did n't light the lantern. You must leave your place. A vessel from St. Geromo was wrecked on the bar. It is lucky that no one was drowned, or you would go to trial. Get into the boat with me; you 'll hear the rest at the Consulate."

The old man grew pale; in fact he had not lighted the lantern that night.

A few days later Skavinski was seen on the deck of a steamer, which was going from Aspinwall to New York. The poor man had lost his place. There opened before him new roads of wandering; the wind had torn that leaf away again to whirl it over lands and seas, to sport with it till satisfied. The old man had failed greatly during those few days, and was bent over; only his eyes were gleaming. On his new road of life he held at his breast his book, which from time to time he pressed with his hand as if in fear that that too might go from him.

FROM·THE·DIARY·OF·A
TUTOR·IN·POZNAN

From the Diary of a Tutor in Poznan

THE lamp, though shaded, roused me, and more than once I saw Mihas still working at two or three o'clock in the morning. His small, fragile figure, dressed only in sleeping clothes, was bent over a book; and in the stillness of the night his drowsy and wearied voice repeated Latin and Greek conjugations mechanically, and in that humdrum voice with which people at church respond to a litany. When I called him to go to bed the boy would answer: "I don't know my lessons yet, Pan Vavry-kevich." I worked out his lessons however from four till eight, and then from nine till twelve o'clock, and did not go to bed myself till I was convinced that he had learned every-thing; but in truth all that he did was too much for him. When he had finished the last lesson the boy had forgotten the first; the conjugations of Greek, Latin, German, and the names of various districts brought his poor head into such confusion that he could not sleep. He crept out from under the quilt then, lighted his lamp, and sat down at the table. When I reproved him, he begged me to let him stay, and he shed tears. I grew so accustomed to those night sittings, to the light of the lamp and to the mumbling of conjugations, that when they were absent I myself could not sleep. Perhaps it was not right for me to permit the child to torture himself beyond his strength; but what was I to do? He had to learn his lessons daily even in some fashion, or he would be expelled from school; and God alone knows what a blow that would have been for Pani Marya, who, left with two orphans after the death of her husband, placed all her hopes on Mihas. The position was well-nigh without escape, for I saw that excessive mental effort was undermining the health of the boy, and might endanger his life. It was needful at the least to strengthen him physically, train him in gymnastics, make him walk a good deal, or ride on horseback; but there was no time for this. The child had so much to do, so much to learn by rote, so much to write every day, that on my conscience I say that there was no time. Every moment required for the recreation, health, and life of the boy was taken by Latin, Greek, and German.

In the morning, when I put his books into the satchel and saw his lean shoulders bending under the weight of those great volumes, my heart simply ached. At times I asked kindness and forbearance for him; but the German pro-

fessors merely answered that I was spoiling and
petting the child, that evidently Mihas was not
working enough, and that he would cry for any
cause. I am weak-breasted myself, solitary, and
sensitive ; hence these reproaches poisoned more
than one moment for me. I knew best whether
Mihas was working enough. He was a child of
medium gifts, but so persevering, and, with all
his mildness, gifted with such strength of character as I have never chanced to meet in another
boy. Poor Mihas was attached to his mother
passionately, blindly ; and since people told him
that she was very unhappy, and sickly, that, if in
addition to other things, he would learn badly it
might kill her, the boy trembled at the thought of
this, and sat whole nights over his books, only
not to kill his mother. He burst into tears when
he received a bad mark ; but it did not come to
the head of any one to inquire why he cried,
or to what terrible responsibility he felt himself
bound at such moments. Indeed, what did any
one care ? I was not spoiling him, nor petting

him ; only I knew him better than others. That I
tried to comfort instead of scolding him for failures was my affair. I have toiled myself in life
no little ; I have suffered hunger and sorrow
enough ; I have not been happy ; I shall not be
happy, and — devils take it ! — I do not even grit
my teeth when I think of this. I do not believe
that life is worth living ; but perhaps for that
very reason I have true sympathy for every
misfortune.

At Mihas's age, when I ran after pigeons on
the streets, or played wagtails under the town-
hall, I had my hours of health and joyousness at
least. A cough did not torment me. When some
one flogged me I cried during the flogging ; but
I was as free as a bird and cared for nothing.
Mihas had not even that. If life had put him
on the anvil and beaten him with its hammer,
he would have gained this much, — that as a boy
he would have laughed heartily at that which
amuses children ; he would have played tricks,
and tired himself in the open air, in the sun-

light.   But I had not before me such a union
of labor with childishness.   On the contrary, I
saw a little boy going to school and coming
home, gloomy, bent, straining under the weight
of books, with wrinkles in the corners of his
eyes, ever holding back, as it were, an outburst
of weeping; therefore, I sympathized with him,
and wished to be a refuge for him.

I am a teacher, though a private one, and I
know not what I should do in the world were
I to lose faith in the value of knowledge and the
benefit which flows from it.   But I think that
study should not be the tragedy of our early
years; that Latin cannot take the place of air
and health; and that a good or bad accent should
not decide the fate and life of children.

I think, too, that the task of instruction is
better accomplished when a boy feels a hand
leading him kindly, and not a foot pressing his
breast and trampling everything which they
teach him at home to love and revere.   I am
such an obscurant that I shall be sure not to

change my opinion in this respect, for I become confirmed in it more and more when I remember my Mihas, whom I loved so sincerely. I taught him six years, first as a governor, and, when he entered the second class, as a private tutor. I had time therefore to grow attached to him. Besides, why should I hide from myself that he was dear to me because he was the son of a being dear to me above all others. She has never known this, and never will. I remember that I am — well, Pan Vavrykevich, a private tutor, and a sickly man in addition; she the daughter of a rich, noble house, a lady to whom I dared not raise my eyes. But since a lone heart, dashed about by life as a mussel is dashed by the waves, must attach itself at last to something, my heart grew to her. How can I help it? And besides, how does that harm her? I do not deprive her of light, any more than I do the sun which warms my weak breast.

I was six years in her house; I was present

at the death of her husband; I saw that she was unhappy, alone, but always as kind as an angel; loving her children, well-nigh a saint in her widowhood; hence I was forced to this feeling. But it is not love on my part, — it is rather my religion.

Mihas reminded me greatly of his mother. More than once when he raised his eyes to me I imagined that I was looking at her. The same delicate features were present, the very same forehead with a shadow of rich hair falling over it, the soft outline of brow, and above all a voice almost identical. In the disposition of the mother and child there was a likeness too, appearing in a certain tendency to exaltation of feelings and views. They belonged both of them to that species of nervous impressionable people, noble and loving, who are capable of the greatest sacrifices, but who in life and in contact with its reality find little happiness, giving, to begin with, more than they can receive in return. That kind of people perish, and I think now that some naturalist might declare them fore-doomed to extinction, for they come into the world with a defect of heart, — they love too much.

Mihas's family was very wealthy at one time, but they loved too much; therefore various storms shattered their fortune, and what re-mained is not indeed want, — it is not even poverty; still in comparison with former days it is moderate. Mihas was the last of the family, therefore Pani Marya loved him not only as her own child, but also as her whole hope for the future. Unfortunately, with the usual blindness of mothers, she saw in him uncommon faculties. The boy was in truth not dull; but he belonged to that class of children whose powers, medium at first, develop only later, together with phys-ical strength and with health. In other condi-tions he might have finished his course in the school and the University, and become a useful worker in any career. In existing conditions he merely tormented himself, and knowing the high

6

opinion which his mother had of his powers, he strained them in vain.

My eyes have seen much in this world, and I have determined to wonder at nothing; but I confess that it was hard for me to believe that there could be a chaos, in which a boy's perseverance, strength of character, and industry would be against him. There is something unhealthy in this; and if words could repay me for sorrow and bitterness, I should say with Hamlet, that there are things in the world which have not been dreamed of by philosophers.

I worked with Mihas as if my own future depended on the marks which he got for his lessons, since my dear pupil and I had one object: not to afflict her, to show good rank, to call out a smile of happiness on her lips. When he succeeded in receiving good marks, the boy came from school radiant and happy. It seemed to me that in such cases he had grown on a sudden, had become erect; his eyes, usually cloudy, laughed now with the unaffected joy of childhood, and gleamed like two coals. He threw from his narrow shoulders his satchel laden with books, and blinking at me said while yet on the threshold : —

" Pan Vavrykevich, Mamma will be satisfied ! I got to-day in geography — guess how many ? "

And when I pretended that I could not guess, he ran to me with a proud mien, and throwing his arms around my neck, said as if in a whisper, but very loud, —

" Five ! truly five ! "

Those were happy moments for us. In the evenings of such days Mihas fell to dreaming, and imagined to himself what would come to pass were he to receive excellent marks all the time, and said half to me, half to himself, —

" On Christmas we will go to Zalesin ; the snow will fall, as is usual in winter ; we 'll go in a sleigh. We 'll arrive at night, but oh ! Mamma will be waiting for me ; she 'll hug me and kiss me, then ask about my marks. I 'll put on a sad face purposely ; then Mamma will read religion excellent, German excellent, Latin excellent, — most excellent ! Oh, Pan Vavrykevich ! "

The poor little boy ! tears were in his eyes ; and I, instead of restraining him, hurried after him with unwearied imagination, and recalled to myself the house in Zalesin, its dignity, its calm, that lofty, noble being who was mistress there, and the happiness which the return of the boy with his excellent rank would bring to her.

I took advantage of such moments, and gave Mihas advice, explaining to him that Mamma cared greatly for his studies, but cared also for his health ; hence he must not cry when I took him to walk, he must sleep as much as I prescribed, and not persist in sitting up at night. The boy, affected by this, embraced me and said, —

" I will obey, my golden Pan. I shall be so well that it will be a wonder to look at me, and I 'll be so fat that neither Mamma nor little Lola will know me."

I too received letters frequently from Pani Marya, recommending me to watch over the health of the child; but I convinced myself daily with despair that that was well-nigh impossible. If the subjects taught were too difficult I could have mended the matter by removing Mihas from the second class to the first; but those subjects, though dry, he understood perfectly. It was not a question of learning, but of time and of that unfortunate German language, which the child could not speak satisfactorily. In this I was powerless, and calculated only that when the holidays came, rest would fill out those breaches in the boy's health made by excessive labor.

If Mihas had been a child of less feeling I should have been less anxious about him; but he felt every failure almost more keenly than he did success. The moments of joy and those *fives* which I have mentioned were rare, unfortunately.

I had so learned to read his face that the

moment he came, I knew at the first glance of the eye that he had not succeeded. " Did you get a bad mark? " I asked.

" I did."

" You did n't know the lesson? "

Sometimes he answered, " I did n't know; " but oftener, " I knew, but I was n't able to tell it."

In fact little Ovitski, the first in the second class, whom I purposely brought in that Mihas might learn with him, said that Mihas received bad marks chiefly because he could not " tongue out."

As the child felt more and more wearied mentally and physically, such failures came oftener. I noticed that after having cried all he wanted he sat down to his lesson quietly and as though he were calm; but in that redoubled energy with which he turned to his tasks there was something both desperate and feverish. Sometimes he went into a corner, pressed his head with both hands, and was silent; the imaginative boy fancied that he was digging a grave under the feet of his darling mother, knew not how to escape this, and felt himself in a vicious circle from which there was no issue.

His night work became more frequent. Fearing that when I woke I would order him to bed, he rose in the dark, silently carried the lamp to the antechamber, lighted it there, and sat down to work. Before I caught him he had passed a number of nights in this way between unheated walls. I had no other resource than to rise, call him to the chamber, and go over all the lessons once more with him, to convince him that he knew them and that he exposed himself to cold without reason. But at last he did n't know himself what he did know. The child lost strength, grew thin, pale, and became more and more despondent. Something happened after a time to convince me that not work alone was exhausting him. Once, while I was explaining to him the history that "An Uncle told his Nephews,"[1] which at the request of Pani Marya I did daily, Mihas sprang up with flashing eyes. I was frightened almost when I saw the inquiring and stern look on his face as he cried, —

"Pan! is that really not a fable? For — "

"Why did you ask, Mihas?" inquired I, with astonishment.

Instead of an answer he gritted his teeth, and burst out at last into such passionate weeping that for a long time I was unable to quiet him.

I inquired of Ovitski touching the cause of this outburst. He either knew not, or would not tell; but I discovered myself. There was no doubt that in the German school the Polish child had to hear many things that wounded his feelings. Such teachings slipped over other boys, leaving no trace except ill-will against the teachers and their whole race; Mihas, a

---

[1] One of Lelewell's histories of Poland.

boy of such uprightness, felt these teachings acutely, but dared not contradict them. Two powers, two voices, obedience to which is the duty of a child, but which for that very reason should be in harmony, were tearing Mihas in two opposite directions. What one power called white, worthy, beloved, the other called a stain vile and ridiculous; what one called virtue the other called vice. Therefore in that separation the boy followed the power to which his heart was attracted, but he had to pretend that he obeyed and took to heart words of the opposite meaning. He had to pretend from morning till night, and to live in that torturing constraint days, weeks, months. What a position for a child!

Mihas's fate was strange. Dramas of life begin later usually, when the first leaves are falling from the tree of youth; for him everything which creates unhappiness — such as moral constraint, concealed regret, trouble of mind, vain efforts, struggling with difficulties, gradual loss of hope — began in the eleventh year of his life. Neither his slight form nor his weak forces could carry those burdens. Days, weeks passed; the poor boy redoubled his efforts, and the result was always less, always more lamentable. The letters of Pani Marya, though sweet, added weight to the burden. "God has gifted you, Mihas, with uncommon capacities," wrote she; "and I trust that you will not disappoint the hopes that I place in you, that you will be a pleasure to me and the country."

When the boy received such a letter the first time he seized my hand spasmodically, and borne away by weeping began to repeat, —

"What shall I do, Pan Vavrykevich, what can I do?"

In truth what could he do? How could he help it that he had n't come into the world with an inborn power over languages, and that he could not pronounce German?

Before the recess at All Saints, the quarterly

return was not very favorable; in three of the most important subjects he had low marks. At his most urgent prayers and entreaties I did not send it to Pani Marya.

" Dear Pan," cried he, putting his hands together, " Mamma does n't know that they give rank at All Saints, and before Christmas the Lord God may take pity on me."

The poor child deluded himself with the hope that he would raise his low rank; and to tell the truth, I deceived myself also. I thought that he would grow accustomed to school routine, that he would grow accustomed to everything, be trained in German, and acquire the accent; above all, that he would need less and less time for his lessons. Had it not been for this I should have written long before to Pani Marya and laid before her the condition of affairs. In fact hopes did not seem vain. Just after All Saints Mihas received three perfect marks, one of which was in Latin. Of all the pupils in the class he alone knew that the perfect of *gaudeo* is *gavisus sum*, and he knew it because he had received before that two perfect marks and had inquired of me what " I rejoice " is in Latin. I thought that the boy would go wild from delight. He wrote a letter to his mother beginning with these words : " Does my beloved Mamma know what the perfect of *gaudeo* is? Surely neither Mamma nor little Lola knows, for in the whole class I was the only one who knew."

Mihas simply adored his mother. From that time he was inquiring of me continually about various perfects and participles. High marks had become the object of his life. But the gleam of fortune was brief. Soon his fatal Polish accent ruined all that effort had built up, and the excessive number of subjects did not permit the child to give each as much time as his strained memory needed. A circumstance caused also an increase of his failures. Mihas and Ovitski forgot to inform me of a certain task in writing, and omitted it.

That passed for Ovitski, for since he stood first the professors did n't even ask him about it; but Mihas received a public admonition in school, with a threat of expulsion.

They thought evidently that he had intentionally concealed the task from me, so as not to do it, and the boy, who was incapable of the least falsehood, had no means of proving his innocence. He might, it is true, say in self-defence that Ovitski had forgotten as well as he; but school honor would not permit such a statement. The Germans answered my assurances with the remark that I encouraged the youngster to laziness. That caused me no little mortification; but the appearance of Mihas increased my anxiety. In the evening of that day I saw that he pressed his head with both hands, and whispered, thinking that I did not hear him, " It pains, it pains, it pains!" The letter from his mother, which came next day, and in which Pani Marya overwhelmed him with tenderness for those good marks, was a fresh blow for him.

"Oh, I am preparing nice consolation for Mamma!" cried he, covering his face with his hands.

Next day, when I put the satchel of books on his shoulders, he tottered and almost fell. I wished to keep him from school, but he said that nothing was the matter; he merely asked me to go with him, for he feared dizziness. He came back in the evening with a new middling mark. He received it for a lesson which he knew perfectly, but according to Ovitski he grew frightened and couldn't say a word. The opinion was confirmed decidedly, — "that he was a boy filled with retrograde principles and instincts, that he was dull and lazy."

With the last two reproaches which had come to his knowledge, he struggled as a drowning man with a wave, — desperately, but in vain.

At last he lost all faith in himself, all confidence in his own powers; he came to the conviction that efforts and labor were useless, that he could n't help learning badly; and at the same time he imagined what his mother would say, what pain it would be for her, and how it might undermine her weak health.

The priest in Zalesin who wrote to him sometimes was very friendly, but incautious. Every letter of his finished with these words: " Let Mihas remember then that not only the joy but the health of his mother depends on his progress in learning and in morality." He remembered too much, for even in sleep he repeated with sad voice: " Mamma, Mamma ! " as if begging her forgiveness.

But when awake, he received lower and lower marks. Meanwhile Christmas was coming quickly, and as to rank it was impossible to be deceived. I wrote to Pani Marya, wishing to forewarn her, told her plainly and positively that the child was weak and overburdened; that in spite of the greatest effort he could not do

his work ; and that probably it would be necessary to take him from school after the holidays,
to keep him in the country, and, above all, to
strengthen his health.   Though I felt in her
answer that her motherly affection was wounded
somewhat, still she wrote like a sensible woman
and a loving mother.   I did not mention this
letter to Mihas, nor the design of taking him
from school, for I feared for him every powerful excitement; I mentioned only that, whatever might happen, his mother knew that he
was working, and she would be able to understand his failure.   That gave him evident
comfort, for he wept long and heartily, — which
had not happened to him for some time.   While
weeping, he repeated : " How much pain I
cause Mamma ! "   Still at the thought that soon
he would return to the country, would see his
mother and little Lola and Father Mashynski, he
laughed through his tears.   I too was in a hurry
to go to Zalesin, for I could hardly bear to look
at the condition of the child.   There the heart

of a mother was waiting for him, and the good will of people, with calm and peace; there knowledge had for him a native air, well wishing, not strange and repellent; there the whole atmosphere was familiar and pure, — the boy's breast might breathe it.

I was looking to the holidays, therefore, as to salvation for the boy; and I counted on my fingers the hours which separated us from them, but which brought more and more new vexation to Mihas. It seemed as though everything had conspired against him. Mihas had received again a public admonition for *demoralizing* others. That was just before the holidays; therefore it had the more significance. How the ambitious and impressionable boy felt the blow, I will not undertake to describe; what chaos must have risen in his mind! Everything was eager in that childish breast, and before his eyes he saw darkness instead of light. He bent then as an ear of grain before the blast. Finally, the face of that boy of eleven took on an expression simply tragic; he looked as if weeping were stopping his throat continually, as if he restrained sobbing by effort; at times his eyes looked like the eyes of a suffering bird; then a wonderful thoughtfulness and drowsiness took possession of him; his motions became as it were unconscious, and his voice mechanically obedient.

When I told him that it was time to walk, he did not resist as formerly, but took his cap and followed me in silence. I should have been content had that been indifference; but I saw that under the appearance of it was hidden an exalted and suffering resignation. He sat at his lessons, performed his tasks as before, but rather from habit. It was evident that, while repeating the conjugations mechanically, he was thinking of something else, or rather he was not thinking of anything. Once, when I asked whether he had finished everything, he answered in a slow voice, and as if sleepily : "I think, Pan, that this is no use." I feared even to mention his mother before him, so as not to fill to overflowing that cup of bitterness from which his childish lips were drinking.

I was more and more alarmed about his health, for he grew thinner and thinner, and at last became almost transparent. The network of delicate veins, which appeared on his temples before when he was greatly excited, had become permanent now. He had grown so beautiful that he was almost like an image. It was painful to look at that childish head, half-angelic, which produced the impression of a withering flower. Apparently it was as if nothing was the matter; but he sank, and lost power. He was able no longer to carry all his books in the satchel; hence I gave only some to him, and carried the others myself, for now I accompanied Mihas to and from school.

At last the holidays were at hand. The horses from Zalesin were waiting two days for us, and Pani Marya's letter, which came with them, stated that all were expecting us there with impatience. " I have heard," concluded Pani Marya, " that it goes hard with you, Mihas; I do not look for high marks; I wish only that the teachers should think with me that you have done what you could, and that with good conduct you have tried to atone for deficient progress."

But the teachers thought differently in every respect; therefore, his rank deceived even that expectation. The last public admonition touched the boy's conduct directly, — that conduct concerning which Pani Marya had such a high opinion. In the judgment of the German professors only that boy conducted himself well who repaid with laughter their jests at the " backwardness of the Poles," at their language and traditions. As a result of these ethical ideas Mihas, as not giving hopes of hearing their explanations in future with profit, and as occupying the place of another for nothing, was expelled from the school.

He brought the sentence in the evening. It

had grown dark in the house, for very heavy snow was falling outside; hence I could not see the face of the child. I saw only that he went to the window, stood in it, and looked without thought, in silence, on the snowflakes whirling in the wind. I did not envy the poor little fellow the thoughts which must have been whirling in his head like the snowflakes outside; but I preferred not to speak to him touching his rank and the sentence. In that way a quarter of an hour passed in bitter silence; but meanwhile it grew dark almost completely. I betook myself to packing the trunk; but seeing that Mihas was standing always at the window, I said at last, —

"What are you doing there, Mihas?"

"Is it true," answered he, in a voice which quivered and hesitated at every syllable, "that Mamma is sitting now with Lola in the green room before the fire, and thinking of me?"

"Perhaps she is. Why does your voice tremble so, — are you sick?"

" Nothing is the matter with me, Pan ; only I am very cold."

I undressed him, and put him to bed at once ; and while undressing him, I looked with compassion on his emaciated knees, and his arms as thin as reed-stalks. I ordered him to drink tea, and covered him with what was possible.

" Are you warmer now ? "

" Oh, yes ! my head aches a little."

Poor head ! it had reason to ache. The suffering child fell asleep soon, and breathed laboriously in his sleep with his narrow breast. I finished packing his and my own things ; then, since I did not feel well, I lay down at once. I blew out the light, and fell asleep almost that moment.

About three o'clock in the morning the lamp and the monotonous well-known muttering waked me. I opened my eyes, and my heart beat unquietly. On the table was the lighted lamp, and at the table sat Mihas over a book.

He was in his shirt only; his cheeks were burning, his eyes partly closed as if for better exertion of his memory; his head was thrown back a little, and his sleepy voice repeated, —

"Subjunctive: Amem, ames, amet, amemus, ametis — "

"Mihas ! "

"Subjunctive: Amem, ames — "

I shook him by the shoulder.

He woke up, and began to blink from astonishment, looking at me as if he did not know me.

"What are you doing? What is the matter, child?"

"Pan," said he, smiling, "I am repeating everything from the beginning; I must get a perfect mark to-morrow."

I took him in my arms, and carried him to bed; his body burned me like fire. Happily the doctor lived in the same house; I brought him at once. He had no need to think long. He held the boy's pulse a moment, then put his hand on his forehead.   Mihas had inflammation of the brain.

Ah, there were many things evidently which could not find place in his head !

His sickness acquired alarming proportions at once.   I sent a dispatch to Pani Marya, and on the next day a violent pull at the bell in the antechamber announced her arrival.   In fact, when I opened the door, I saw through the black veil her face, pale as linen.   Her fingers rested on my shoulder with uncommon force, and her whole soul rushed out through her eyes, which were fixed on me, when she asked briefly, —

" Is he alive ? "

" He is.   The doctor says that he is better."

She threw aside the veil, on which hoar frost had settled from her breath, and hurried to the boy's chamber.   I had lied.   Mihas was alive, it is true ; but he was not better.   He did not even know his mother when she sat near him, and took his hand.   Only when I had placed fresh ice on his head did he begin to blink, and look with effort at the face bent above him. His mind made an evident effort, struggling with fever and delirium; his lips quivered, he smiled once and a second time, and whispered at last, —

"Mamma!"

She seized both his hands, and sat in that way at his side a number of hours, not casting aside even her travelling costume. Only when I turned her attention to this, did she say, —

"True. I forgot to remove my hat."

When she took it off, my heart was oppressed with a wonderful feeling: among the blond hair adorning that young and beautiful head, silver threads were gleaming thickly. Three days ago, perhaps, there were none there.

She changed compresses for the boy herself, and gave him the medicine. Mihas followed her with his eyes wherever she moved, but again he did not recognize her. In the evening the fever increased; he declaimed in his raving the ballad about " Jolkyevski from Nyemtse-vich ; " at times he spoke in the language of teaching ; again he conjugated various Latin verbs. I left the room repeatedly, for I could not listen to this. While in good health, he had been learning in secret to serve at Mass, wishing to give his mother a surprise when he came home ; and now a shiver passed through me when in the stillness of the evening I heard that boy of eleven years repeating before his death with a monotonous and expiring voice : " Deus meus, quare me repulisti, et quare tristis incedo dum affligit me inimicus [My God, why hast Thou rejected me, and why am I walking in grief while my enemy afflicts me] ! "

I cannot tell what a tragic impression these words produced. It was Christmas eve. From the street came the hum of people and the tinkling of sleigh bells. The town had taken on a holiday and joyful exterior. When it had grown dark completely, through the windows on the other side of the street was to be

seen an evergreen-tree gleaming with lights,
and hung with glittering gold and silver nuts,
and around it the heads of children bright
and dark, with locks flowing in the air, jump-
ing as if on springs. The windows were
gleaming, and the whole interior resounded
with cries of delight and wonder. Among
the voices coming from the street there were
none except joyous ones, and gladness had
become universal; our boy alone repeated, as
if with great sorrow: "Deus meus, Deus meus,
quare me repulisti?" At the gate, boys halted
with a little booth, and soon the song reached
us: "He is lying in the manger, who will run?"
Christmas night was approaching, and we trembled lest it should be a night of death.

After a while it seemed to us, however, that
the boy had become conscious, for he began
to call Lola and his mother; but that was of
short duration. His quick breathing stopped
at times altogether. There was no cause for
self-deception; that little soul was already only

half with us.   His mind had flown away, and
now he was going himself into some dark distance and endlessness; already he saw no one,
and felt nothing, — not even the head of his
mother, which was lying as if dead at his feet.
He had grown indifferent, and looked no longer
at us.   Every breath of his bosom removed him,
and as it were pushed him out into the darkness.   Disease was quenching spark after spark
of his life.   The hands of the child lying on
the coverlet were outlined on it with heavy
helplessness, the mark of death; his nose became sharp, and his face took on a certain cold
seriousness.   His breath became quicker, and at
last was like the ticking of a watch.   A moment
more, another sigh, and the last grain of sand
was to fall from the hourglass; the end was
inevitable.

About midnight it seemed to us decisively
that he was dying, for he began to rattle and
groan like a man into whose mouth water is
flowing, and then he was silent suddenly.   But

the glass which the doctor placed at his lips was covered yet with the mist of respiration. An hour later the fever decreased all at once; we thought that he was saved. The doctor himself had some hope. Poor Pani Marya grew faint.

In the course of two hours he was better and better. Toward morning, since that was the fourth night which I had spent near the boy without sleeping, and since a cough was stifling me with growing violence, I went to the ante-room, lay on a straw bed, and fell asleep. The voice of Pani Marya roused me. I thought that she was calling me, but in the stillness of night I heard clearly, "Mihas! Mihas!" The hair stood on my head, for I understood the terrible accent with which she cried to the child; before I sprang up, however, she ran in herself, holding the light in her hand, and whispered with quivering lips, —

"Mihas — is dead!"

I ran in a breath to the boy's bed. So it was.

The head fallen back on the pillow, the mouth open, the eyes fixed without motion on one point, and the rigidity of every feature, left not the least doubt : Mihas was dead.

I covered him with the quilt, which his mother, in springing away from the bed, had pulled from his emaciated body. I closed his eyes, and then I had to rub Pani Marya a long time.

The first of the holidays passed in preparations for the funeral, which for me was terrible, for Pani Marya would not leave the corpse, and she was fainting continually. She fainted when men came to take the dimensions of the coffin, again when they began to prepare the body, finally when the catafalque was put up. Her despair was in continual clash with the indifference of the undertaker's assistants, accustomed as they were to similar sights, and passed almost into raving. She herself put shavings in the coffin under the satin, repeating, as if in a fever, that the child's head would be too low. And Mihas was lying meanwhile on his bed, in his new uniform and white gloves, rigid, indifferent, and calm. We placed the body at last in the coffin, put that on the catafalque, and set two rows of candles around it. The room in which the poor child had conjugated so many Latin verbs and worked out so many lessons had changed as it were into a chapel, for the closed windows did not admit sunshine, and the yellow, flickering light of the candles gave the walls a certain church-like and solemn appearance. Never since Mihas had received his last high mark had I seen his face so full of contentment. His delicate profile turned to the ceiling was smiling, as if in that eternal reaction of death the boy had pleased himself and felt happy. The flickering of the candles gave to his face and to that smile an appearance of life and sleep.

By degrees those of the boys his colleagues who had not gone home for the holidays began to assemble. The eyes of the children grew wide with wonder at sight of the candles, the catafalque, and the coffin. Perhaps the dignity and importance of their colleague astonished the little scholars. Not long since he was among them, bending like them under the weight of a satchel overladen with German books; he received bad marks, was scolded and admonished publicly; each might pull his hair or his ears. But now he lay there above them, dignified, calm, surrounded with light; all approached him with respect and with a certain awe, — and even Ovitski, though the first scholar, did not mean much before him. The boys, pushing each other with their elbows, whispered that now he cared for nothing; that even if " Herr Inspector " had come, he would not spring up nor be frightened, but would continue to smile quietly as before. " He can do just as he likes," said they; "he can shout as he likes, and talk to little angels with wings on their shoulders."

Thus they approached the rows of candles, and asked eternal rest for Mihas.

The next day the coffin was covered with the lid, fastened with nails, and taken to the cemetery, where lumps of sand mixed with snow soon concealed it from my eyes forever. To-day, as I write, almost a year has passed from that time; but I remember thee, and I mourn for thee, my little Mihas, my flower withered untimely. I do not know where thou art, or if thou dost hear me; I know only that thy old teacher's cough is increasing, that the world is more oppressive for him, that he is more lonely, and may go soon to the place whither thou hast gone.

A Comedy of Errors.

FIVE or six years since it happened that oil springs were discovered in a certain place in Mariposa County, California. The enormous profits which such springs yield in Nevada and other States, induced a number of men to form a company for the purpose of working the newly-discovered springs. They brought in various machines, — pumps, engines, ladders, barrels, kegs, drills, and kettles ; they built houses for laborers, and called the place Struck Oil. After a certain time a desert and uninhabited neighborhood, which a year before was inhabited only by coyotes, became a settlement composed of a number of tens of houses occupied by several hundred laborers.

Two years later, Struck Oil was called Struck Oil City. In fact it was a " city " in the full meaning of that term. I beg the reader to note that there were living in the city a shoemaker, a tailor, a carpenter, a blacksmith, a butcher, and a doctor, — a Frenchman, who in his time had shaved beards in France, but for the rest a " learned man," and harmless, which in an American doctor means a great deal.

The doctor, as happens very often in small American towns, kept also a drug store and post-office ; therefore he had a triple practice. He was as harmless an apothecary as he was a doctor, for it was possible to buy only two kinds of medicine in his drug store, — sugar sirup and leroa.[1] This quiet and mild old man said usually to his patients, —

"You need not fear my prescriptions, for when I give medicine to a patient I always take the same dose myself; I understand that if it will not hurt me while in health it will not harm a sick man. Is n't that true?"

"True," answered the reassured citizen, to whom somehow it did not occur that it was not only the duty of a doctor to avoid injuring a sick man, but to help him.

Monsieur Dasonville, such was the doctor's name, believed especially in the miraculous effects of leroa. More than once at meetings he removed the hat from his head, and turning to the public said, —

"Ladies and gentlemen, convince yourselves concerning leroa. I am eighty-four years of age and use leroa every day. Look at me, I have not one gray hair on my head."

The ladies and gentlemen might discover

[1] Leroa is, no doubt, the French *Le roi*, the King.

that the doctor had not one gray hair; but then he had no hair at all, for his head was as bald as a lamp globe. But since discoveries of that kind contributed in no way to the growth of Struck Oil City, no one made them.

Meanwhile Struck Oil City grew and grew. At the expiration of two years a branch railroad was built to it. The city had its elective officers also. The doctor, whom everybody loved, was chosen judge, as a representative of the intelligence; the shoemaker, a Polish Jew, Mr. Davis (David was his real name) was chosen sheriff, that is, chief of the police, which was composed of the sheriff and no one else; they built a schoolhouse, for the management of which a "schoolma'am" was imported on purpose, — a maiden born before man reckoned time, and who had an eternal toothache; finally, the first hotel rose, and was named United States Hotel.

"Business" was lively beyond measure.

The export of oil brought good profit. It was noticed that Mr. Davis had put out before his shop a glass showcase, like those which adorn the shoeshops in San Francisco. At the following meeting the inhabitants thanked Mr. Davis publicly for this "new ornament to the city." Mr. Davis answered with the modesty of a great citizen, "Thank you! thank you!"

Where there is a judge and a sheriff there are lawsuits. These require writing and paper. Therefore, on the corner of First and Coyote street there arose a "stationery," that is a paper shop, in which were sold also political daily papers and caricatures, one of which represented President Grant in the form of a man milking a cow, which in her turn represented the United States. The duties of the sheriff did not enjoin on him at all to forbid the sale of such pictures, for that does not pertain to the police.

But this was not the end yet. An American

city cannot be without a newspaper. At the end of the second year, therefore, a paper appeared called the "Saturday Weekly Review," which had as many subscribers as there were inhabitants in Struck Oil City. The editor of that paper was its publisher, printer, business manager, and carrier. The last duty came to him the more easily, since in addition to his business he kept cows, and had to deliver milk every morning at the houses of citizens. But this did not prevent him in any way from beginning his leading political articles with the words: "If our miserable President of the United States had followed the advice which we gave him in the last number," etc.

As we see, nothing was wanting in blessed Struck Oil City. Besides, since men who work at getting oil are not distinguished either by the violence or rude manners which mark golddiggers, it was peaceful in the city. No man had a fight with another; there was not a word spoken of "lynching;" life flowed on calmly.

One day was as much like another as one drop
of water is like another. In the morning every
man occupied himself with " business ; " in the
evening the inhabitants burned sweepings on
the street ; and, if there was no meeting, they
went to bed, knowing that on the following
evening they would burn sweepings again.

But the sheriff was annoyed by one thing, —
he could not break the citizens from firing at
wild geese which flew over the place in the
evening. The laws of the city prohibited
shooting on the streets. " If this were some
mangy little village," said the sheriff, " I
would n't say anything ; but in such a great
city to have pif ! paf ! pif ! paf ! is very unbe-
coming."

The citizens listened, nodded, and answered,
" Oh, yes ; " but in the evening when on the
blushing sky the white and gray lines appeared,
stretching from the mountains to the ocean,
every man forgot his promise, seized his cara-
bine, and shooting began in good earnest.

Mr. Davis might, it is true, have summoned each trespasser before the judge, and the judge could punish him with a fine; but it must not be forgotten that the offenders were in case of sickness patients of the doctor, and in case of broken shoes customers of the sheriff; since then hand washes hand, hand did not offend hand. Hence, it was as peaceful in Struck Oil City as in heaven; still, those halcyon days had a sudden end.

A man who kept a grocery was inflamed with mortal hatred toward a woman who kept a grocery, and the woman with hatred toward him.

Here it may be needful to explain what that is which in America is called " a grocery." A grocery is a place in which they sell goods of all kinds. In a grocery you can find flour, caps, cigars, brooms, buttons, rice, sardines, stockings, ham, garden seeds, coats, pantaloons, lamp chimneys, axes, crackers, crockery, paper-collars, dried fish; in a word, everything which a man can use.

At first there was only one grocery in Struck
Oil City. It was kept by a German named
Hans Kasche. He was a phlegmatic German
from Prussia, thirty-five years of age, and had
staring eyes; he was not fat, but portly; he
went about always in his shirt-sleeves, and
never let the pipe out of his mouth. He knew
as much English as was needful in business;
more than that not a toothful. But he man-
aged his business well, so that in a year people
said in Struck Oil City that he was worth
several thousand dollars.

On a sudden, however, a second grocery was
opened.

And marvellous thing! a German man kept
the first grocery, a German woman established
the second. *Kunegunde und Eduard, Eduard
und Kunegunde!* Straightway a war was begun
between the two sides; it began from this, — that
Miss Neumann, or, as she called herself, " Miss
Newman," gave at her opening " lunch " pan-
cakes baked from flour mixed with soda and

alum. She would have injured herself in the highest degree by this in the opinion of the citizens,
were it not that she stated, and then proved
by witnesses, that, as her flour had not been
opened, she had bought this from Hans Kasche.
It came out then that Hans Kasche was an
envious man and a villain, who wished from
the very first to ruin his rival in public estima-
tion. Of course, it was to be foreseen that the
two groceries would be rivals; but no one could
foresee that the rivalry would pass into such
terrible personal hatred. Soon that hatred increased to such a degree that Hans burned
sweepings only when the wind blew the smoke
from his shop to that of his rival; and the
rival had no other name for Hans than
" Dutchman," which he considered as the
greatest insult.

At the beginning, the citizens laughed at
both, all the more since neither of them knew
English; gradually, however, through daily
relations with the groceries, two parties were

formed in the city, — the Hansites and the Newmanites, who began to look at each other askance, which might have injured the happiness and peace of Struck Oil City, and brought dreadful complications for the future. Mr. Davis, the profound politician, was anxious to cure the evil at its source; hence he strove to reconcile the German woman with the German man. More than once he stood in the middle of the street, and said to them in their native tongue, —

"Well, why do you fight? Is it because you do not patronize the same shoemaker? I have such shoes now that in all San Francisco there are no better."

"It is useless to recommend shoes to him who will be barefoot before long," replied Miss Newman, sourly.

"I do not win credit with my feet," answered Hans, phlegmatically.

And it is necessary to know that Miss Newman, though a German, had really pretty feet;

therefore such a taunt filled her heart with mortal anger.

In the city the two parties began to raise the question of Hans and Miss Newman; but since no man in America can obtain justice against a woman, the majority inclined to the side of Miss Newman.

Soon Hans saw that his grocery was barely paying expenses.

But Miss Newman too did not win such brilliant victories, for soon all the married women in the city took the side of Hans, for they noticed that their husbands made purchases too often from the fair German, and sat too long at each purchase.

When no one was in either shop, Hans and Miss Newman stood in their doors, one opposite the other, casting mutual glances filled with venom. Miss Newman sang at such times to herself to the air of " Mein lieber Augustin," —

" Dutchman, Dutchman, Du-u-u-tchman, Du-u-u-tch-
        man ! "

Hans looked at her feet, at her figure, at her face with an expression such as he would have had in looking at a coyote killed outside the city; then, bursting into demoniacal laughter, he exclaimed, —

"*Mein Gott!*"

Hatred in that phlegmatic man rose to such a pitch that when he appeared at the door in the morning, and Miss Newman was not there, he was as fidgety as if he missed something.

There would have been active collisions between them long before, were it not that Hans was sure of defeat in every official decision, and that all the more since Miss Newman had on her side the editor of the "Saturday Weekly Review." Hans convinced himself of this when he spread the report that Miss Newman wore a false bust. That was even likely, for in America it is a common custom. But on the following week there appeared in the "Saturday Weekly Review" a thundering article, in which the editor, speaking generally of the slanders of

"Dutchmen," ended with the solemn assurance "of one well informed" that the bust of a certain slandered lady is genuine.

From that day forward Hans drank black coffee every morning instead of white, for he would take milk no longer from that editor; but to make up for the loss, Miss Newman took milk for two. Moreover, she ordered at the dressmaker's a robe, which, by the cut of its bosom, proved convincingly to all that Hans was a slanderer.

Hans felt defenceless before woman's cunning; meanwhile his opponent, standing before her shop every morning, sang louder and louder, —

"Dutchman, Dutchman, Du-u-u-u-tchman, Du-u-u-u-tch-man!"

"What am I to do?" thought Hans. "I have wheat poisoned for rats; let me poison her hens with it? No, the justice would sentence me to pay for them. But I know what to do."

And in the evening Miss Newman, to her great astonishment, saw Hans carrying bunches of wild sunflowers, and laying them out as if in a row under the barred window of his cellar. "I am curious to know what is coming," thought she to herself, — "surely something against me." Meanwhile night came. Hans had put the sunflowers in two rows, so that only between them was there an open path to the window of the cellar; then he brought some object covered with cloth, and turned his back to Miss Newman. He took the cloth from the mysterious object, covered it with sunflower leaves, then approached the wall, and began to make certain letters on it.

Miss Newman was dying with curiosity. "Of course he is writing something about me," thought she; "but only let all go to sleep, I'll walk over there and see, even if it kills me."

When Hans had finished his work, he went upstairs, and soon after put his light out. Then Miss Newman threw on her wrapper quickly, put slippers on her bare feet, and went across the street. When she came to the sunflowers, she went straight to the window, wishing to read the writing on the wall. Suddenly the eyes went up into her head; she threw back the upper half of her body, and from her mouth came with pain, "Ei! ei!" then the despairing cry, "Help! help!"

The window above was raised. "*Was ist das?*" was heard in the quiet voice of Hans. "*Was ist das?*"

"Cursed Dutchman," screamed the lady, "you have murdered me, destroyed me! You'll hang to-morrow. Help! help!"

"I'll come down right away," said Hans.

In fact he appeared after a while with a light in his hand. He looked at Miss Newman, who was as if spiked to the earth; then he caught his sides, and began to laugh.

"What is this? Miss Newman? Ha! ha! ha! Good evening, Miss Newman! Ha! ha! ha! I put out a skunk-trap, and caught Miss

Newman. Why did you come to look at my cellar? I wrote a notice on the wall to keep away. Scream now; let people crowd up here; let all see that you come at night to look into the Dutchman's cellar. *O mein Gott!* Cry away; but stay there till morning. Good-by, Miss Newman, good-by!"

The position of Miss Newman was dreadful. If she screamed, people would collect, — she would be compromised; if she did n't cry, she 'd stay all night caught in a trap, and next day make a show of herself. And there her foot was paining her more and more. Her head whirled around; the stars were confused with one another, and the moon with the ominous face of Hans Kasche. She fainted.

" *Herr Je!* " cried Hans to himself, " if she dies, they will lynch me in the morning without trial; " and the hair rose on his head from terror.

There was no help for it. Hans looked for his key as quickly as possible to open the trap; but it was n't easy to open it, for Miss Newman's wrapper was in the way. He had to put it aside somewhat; and, in spite of all his hatred and fear, Hans could n't help casting an eye at the feet beautiful as if of marble, — those feet of his enemy lighted by the red gleam of the moon.

A man might say that in his hatred then there was compassion. He opened the trap quickly; and, since Miss Newman made no movement, he took her in his arms, and carried her to her dwelling. On the way he felt compassion again. Then he went home, and could n't close an eye all that night.

Next morning Miss Newman did not appear before her grocery to sing, —

" Dutchman, Dutchman, Du-u-u-u-tchman, Du-u-u-u-tch-man ! "

Maybe that she was ashamed, and maybe that in silence she was forging revenge.

It turned out that she was forging revenge. On the evening of that same day the editor of

the "Saturday Weekly Review" challenged Hans
to fight with fists, and at the very beginning of
the battle he gave him a black eye. But Hans,
brought to despair, gave so many terrible blows
to the editor that, after a short and vain oppo-
sition, the editor fell his whole length, crying,
" Enough ! Enough ! "

It is unknown by what means, — for it was n't
through Hans, — the whole city heard about the
night adventure of Miss Newman. After the
fight with the editor, compassion for his enemy
vanished again from Hans's heart, and there
remained only hatred.

Hans Kasche had a foreboding that some un-
expected blow would strike him from the hated
hand. In fact he did not have to wait long.
Grocery-keepers paste up on their shops adver-
tisements of various articles entitled usually
" Notice." Besides, it is necessary to know that
usually they sell ice to saloon-keepers, — without
ice no American drinks either whiskey or beer.
All at once Hans noticed that people stopped

taking ice of him.   The immense blocks,
which he had brought by railroad and put in
the cellar, thawed ; there was a loss of several
dollars.   Why was that?   How was it?   Hans
saw that even his partisans bought ice every day
from Miss Newman ; he did n't know what this
meant, especially since he had not quarrelled
with a single saloon-keeper.   He determined to
clear up the matter.

"Why don't you take ice of me?" asked he,
in broken English, of a saloon-keeper, Peters,
who was just passing his grocery.

"Because you don't keep any."

"Why don't I keep any?"

"How do I know?"

"*Aber* I keep it."

"But what is that?" asked the saloon-keeper,
pointing to the notice stuck up on the grocery.

Hans looked, and grew green from rage ;
from his "Notice" some one has scratched out
the letter *t* from the middle of the word, in
consequence of which "Notice" became "No
ice."

"*Donnerwetter!*" screamed Hans, and all blue and trembling, he rushed to Miss Newman's grocery.

"That 's scoundrelism!" cried he, foaming at the mouth. "Why did you scratch out a letter in the middle from me?"

"What did I scratch out from you in the middle?" asked Miss Newman, with a look of innocence.

"The letter *t*, I say. You scratched out *t* from me! *Aber* Gottam! this cannot last longer. You must pay me for that ice, Miss Newman! Gottam! Gottam!"

And losing his ordinary cool blood, he began to roar like a madman, whereupon Miss Newman fell to screaming; people flew together in a crowd.

"Help!" cried Miss Newman. "The Dutchman is raving! He says that I scratched something out of his middle, and I have n't scratched anything from him. What was I to scratch? I have n't scratched anything. In

God's name! I 'd scratch his eyes out if I could, but nothing else. I am a poor lone woman! he 'll kill me, he 'll murder me!"

Screaming in this way, she covered herself with hot tears. The Americans did n't know, in fact, what the question was; but Americans will not endure woman's tears; therefore they took the German by the neck, and through the door with him. He wanted to resist; little use in that! he flew as out of a sling, flew through the street, flew through his own door, and dropped at full length.

A week later there hung an immense painted sign on his shop. The sign represented an ape in a striped dress, with a white apron and shoulder straps, — in one word, exactly like Miss Newman. Underneath stood an inscription in great golden letters, —

"GROCERY UNDER THE APE."

The people collected to look at it. Their laughter brought Miss Newman to the door.

She came out, looked, grew pale, but without losing presence of mind called out at once, —

"Grocery under the ape? No wonder, for Hans Kasche lives over the grocery. Ha!"

The blow however pierced her to the heart. In the afternoon she heard how crowds of children passing the grocery on their way from school, and stopping before the sign, cried, —

"Oh, that's Miss Newman! Good evening, Miss Newman!"

This was too much. In the evening when the editor came to her, she said to him, —

"That ape means me, I know that; but I will not give up my own. He must take down that ape and lick it off before me with his own tongue."

"What do you wish to do, Miss Newman?"

"I'll go this minute to the judge."

"How this minute?"

"To morrow."

In the morning she went out, and walking up to Hans. said. —

"Listen to me, Mr. Dutchman, I know that that ape means me. Come with me to the judge. We'll see what he'll say to this."

"He will say that I am free to paint on my shop what I like."

"We'll see about that very soon." Miss Newman was hardly able to breathe.

"But how do you know that that ape means you?"

"Conscience tells me. Come, come to the judge; if not, the sheriff will take you in chains."

"Very well, I'll go," said Hans, certain of victory.

They shut up their groceries and went, meditating for themselves along the road. Only when they were at Judge Dasonville's door did they remember that neither of them knew English enough to explain the affair. What were they to do? The sheriff, being a Polish Jew, knew German and English. They went to the sheriff; but the sheriff was just getting into his wagon to drive off.

"Go to the devil!" said he, in a hurry. "The whole city is disturbed by you! You wear the same shoes whole years! I am going for lumber. Good by!" And he drove away.

Hans put his hands on his hips. "You must wait till to-morrow," said he, phlegmatically.

"I wait? I'd die first, unless you take down the ape."

"I won't take it down."

"You'll hang, Dutchman. We'll do without the sheriff. The judge knows already what the matter is."

"We'll go without the sheriff," said the German.

Miss Newman was mistaken, however. The judge was the only man in the whole city who didn't know one word of their quarrels. The old man was busy in preparing his leroa, and thought he was saving the world. He received them as he received every one usually, with kindness and politely.

" Show your tongues, my children ! " said he ;
" I will prescribe for you this minute."

Both waved their hands in sign that they
did n't want medicine.   Miss Newman repeated,
" Not that, not that ! "

" What then ? "

They interrupted each other.   When Hans
said a word the lady said ten.   At last she
fell upon the idea of pointing to her heart as a
sign that Hans had offended her mortally.

" I understand !   I understand now ! " cried
the doctor.

Then he opened his book and began to write.
He asked Hans how old he was, — thirty-six.   He
asked the lady ; she did n't remember exactly, —
something about twenty-five.   All right !   What
were their names?   Hans, — Lora.   All right !
What was their occupation?   They kept grocery.
All right !   Then other questions.   Neither of
them understood, but they answered yes.   The
doctor nodded.   All was over.

He stopped writing, rose on a sudden, to the

great astonishment of Lora put his arm around her waist and kissed her. She took this as a good omen, and went home full of rosy hopes.

On the road she said to Hans, " I 'll show you ! "

" You 'll show some one else," said the German, calmly.

Next morning the sheriff passed in front of the groceries. The German man and woman were before their own doors. Hans was smoking his pipe, and Miss Newman was singing :

"Dutchman, Dutchman, Du-u-u-u-tchman, Du-u-u-u-tchman ! "

" Do you want to go to the justice ? " asked the sheriff.

" We have been there."

" Well, and what ? "

" My dear sheriff ! My dear Mr. Davis ! " cried Miss Newman, " go and find out. I just need some shoes ; and speak a word for me to the justice. You see I am a poor, lone woman."

The sheriff went, and came back in a quarter

of an hour.   But it is unknown why he was surrounded by a crowd of people.

"Well, what? how was it?" both began to inquire.

"All is right," said the sheriff.

"Well, what did the justice do?"

"Well, what harm had he to do?   He married you."

"Married!"

"Well, don't people marry?"

If a thunderbolt had burst on a sudden, Hans and Miss Newman would n't have been astonished to that degree.   Hans stared, opened his mouth, hung out his tongue, and looked like a fool at Miss Newman; Miss Newman stared, opened her mouth, hung out her tongue, and looked like a fool at Hans.   They were petrified. Then both screamed : —

"Am I to be his wife?"

"Am I to be her husband?"

"Murder! murder! Never! A divorce right away! I won't have a marriage!"

"No, it's I that won't have it!"

"I'll die first! murder! A divorce, a divorce!"

"My dears," said the sheriff, quietly, "what good will screaming do you? The judge marries, but the judge cannot divorce. What's the use in screaming? Are you millionnaires from San Francisco, to get a divorce; or don't you know what that costs? Ai! What's the use in screaming? I have nice children's shoes for sale cheap. Good-by!"

When he had said that he went away. The people too went away laughing; the newly married remained alone.

"That Frenchman," cried the married lady, "did this purposely, because we are Germans."

"Richtig [correct]," answered Hans.

"But we'll go for a divorce."

"I first! You took me that *t* from the middle."

"No! I'll go first! You caught me in the trap."

"I don't want you."

"I can't bear you."

They separated and closed their shops.   She
sat at home thinking all day; he sat at home.
Night came.   Night brought no rest; neither
could think of sleep.   They lay down, but their
eyes would not close.   He thought, "My wife
is sleeping over there;" she, "My husband is
sleeping over there."   And some strange feeling rose in their hearts.   It was hatred, anger,
together with a feeling of loneliness.   Besides,
Hans began to think of the ape on his grocery.
How keep it there when it was now a caricature
of his wife?   It seemed to him that he had
played a very ugly trick when he gave an order
to paint the ape.   But again that Miss Newman!   But he hates her; through her his ice
thawed; he caught her during moonlight in a
trap.   Here again those outlines came to his
mind, which he saw in the moonlight.   "But,
really, she is a brave girl," thought he.   "But she
can't stand me and I can't stand her.   That's a
position!   *Ach! Herr Gott!* I am married.

To whom? To Miss Newman! And here a divorce costs so much that the whole grocery would n't pay for it."

"I am the wife of that Dutchman," said Miss Newman to herself. "I 'm no longer a maiden, — that is, I mean to say single, — but married! To whom? To Kasche, who caught me in a trap. It is true that he took me up and brought me home. And how strong he is! Just took me up. — What 's that? Is there some noise here?"

There was no noise whatever; but Miss Newman began to be afraid, though up to that time she had never been afraid.

"But if he should dare now — O God —" Then she added, with a voice in which was heard a certain strange note of disappointment, "But he won't dare. He —"

With all that her fear increased. "That 's always the way with a lone woman," thought she. "If there was a man in the house it would be safer. I 've heard of murders in the neigh-

borhood [Miss Newman had not heard of mur-
ders]. I swear that if they kill me here — Ah,
that Kasche! that Kasche! has stopped my
road. But it's necessary to take measures for
a divorce."

Thinking thus she turned sleeplessly on her
wide American bed, and really felt very lonely.
She sprang up again suddenly. This time her
fear had a real foundation. In the silence of
night was heard distinctly the pounding of a
hammer.

"Heaven!" cried Miss Newman, "they are
breaking into my grocery!"

She sprang out of bed and ran to the window;
but when she looked out she was at rest in a
moment. By the light of the moon a ladder
was to be seen, and on it the portly white figure
of Hans drawing with the hammer the nails
fastening the sign of the ape.

Miss Newman opened the window quietly.

"He is taking down the ape, — that is honorable on his part," thought she. And she felt all

at once as if something were melting around her heart.

Hans drew out the nails one after another. The plate fell to the ground with a rattle; then he came down, took off the frame, folded up the plate in his strong hands, and began to remove the ladder.

Miss Newman followed him with her eyes. The night was quiet and warm.

" Herr Hans," called she, in a low voice.

" You are not sleeping? " answered Hans, in an equally low tone.

" No; good evening, Herr."

" Good evening."

" What are you doing? "

" Taking down the ape."

" Thank you, Herr Hans."

A moment of silence.

" Herr Hans," said the maiden again.

" What is it, Fräulein Lora? "

" We must arrange for the divorce."

" Yes."

"To-morrow?"

"To-morrow."

A moment of silence; the moon was laughing, the dogs not barking.

"Herr Hans!"

"What, Fräulein Lora?"

"I should like to have that divorce right away." Her voice had a melancholy tone.

"I too, Fräulein Lora." His voice was sad.

"So there should be no delay, you see."

"Better not delay."

"The sooner we talk the question over the better."

"The better, Fräulein Lora."

"Then we may talk it over right away."

"If you permit."

"Then come over here."

"Only let me dress."

"No need of ceremony."

The door below opened. Herr Hans vanished in the darkness, and after a while found himself in the young woman's chamber, which was quiet, warm, tidy. She wore a white dressing gown, and was enchanting.

"I am listening to you," said Hans, with a broken, soft voice.

" But, you see, I should like very much to get a divorce, but — I am afraid somebody on the street will see us."

" But it is dark in the window," said Hans.

" Ah, that is true ! " answered she.

Thereupon began a conversation concerning divorce which does not belong to this narrative.

Peace returned to Struck Oil City.

BARTEK
THE
VICTOR

BARTEK THE VICTOR

I.

MY hero was Bartek Slovik;[1] but since he
had the habit of staring when any one
spoke to him, his neighbors called him Bartek
the Starer. In truth he had little in common
with the nightingale; on the contrary, his
mental qualities and his real Homeric sim-
plicity gained for him the nickname of Bartek
the Stupid. The last name was the most

[1] Slovik means in Polish "nightingale."

popular, and without doubt is the only one
that will pass into history, though Bartek had
a fourth, an official name. Since the Polish
words "chlovyek"[1] and "slovik" present no
difference to the German ear, and since the
Germans love to translate, in the name of civilization, barbarous Slav names into a more
cultured language, the following conversation
took place in its time while they were register-
ing the army list : —

"What is thy name?" asked the officer of
Bartek.

"Slovik."

"Shloik? Ach, ja! Gut!"

And the officer wrote down, "Mensch"
(man).

Bartek came from the village of Pognembin;
there are very many villages of that name in the
Principality of Poznan, and in other lands of

[1] Chlovyek means "man." Owing to German inca-
pacity to distinguish Slav sounds, the officer confounds
the word which means man with that which means
nightingale.

the former Commonwealth. Besides his land, cottage, and two cows he had a pied horse, and a wife Magda. Thanks to such a concurrence of circumstances, he could live quietly and according to the wisdom contained in the following lines : —

"A horse a pied one, and a wife Magda,
What God is to give He will give in His way."

In fact, his life arranged itself completely as God gave, and when God gave war Bartek was grieved not a little. Notice came that he must join the regiment ; he had to go from his cottage and land, and leave everything to the care of the woman. The people in Pognembin were on the whole poor enough. Bartek used to go to the mill to work in winter, and in that way helped his housekeeping ; but what now? Who knows when the war with the French will be over? When Magda read the ticket of summons, she began to curse : "May they — may they be blinded ! Though thou art stupid, Bartek, I am sorry for thee ; the French, too, will not let thee pass; they will cut thy head off, or something."

Bartek embraced his wife, his ten-year old Franek; then he spat, made the sign of the cross, went out of the cottage, and Magda after him. They did not part with an overflow of feeling. She and the boy sobbed. Bartek repeated, "Now be quiet, now," and they found themselves on the road. There they saw that the same visitation had come to all Pognembin. The whole village had come out; the road was crowded with men called to the war. They were going to the railroad station, and women, children, old men, and dogs were accompanying them. It was heavy on the hearts of the summoned men. Pipes were hanging from the mouths of only a few of the younger ones; some were already drunk, to begin with; some were singing, with hoarse voices, —

> "Skrynetski's hands and gold rings
> Will not wield a sabre at the war."

A few Germans, too, of the Pognembin colonists were singing from fear "Die Wacht am
Rhein." All that crowd, motley and many-
colored, in the midst of which the bayonets of
the police were glittering, was pushing forward
along the fences with cries, uproar, and hustling.
The women were holding their "soldier-boys"
by the neck, and weeping; one old woman,
showing a yellow tooth, shook her fist at something in space; another was cursing, "May
the Lord God pay you for our tears!" Cries
were heard of "Franek! Kasek! Jozek! farewell!" Dogs are barking. The bell on the
church is ringing. The parish priest is reading
by himself prayers for the dying, for not all of
those who are going now to the station will return. War takes them all, but war will not give
them back. The ploughs are rusting in the fur-
rows, for Pognembin has declared war against
France. Pognembin would not recognize the
preponderance of Napoleon III., and took the
cause of the Spanish succession to heart. The

sound of the bell conducted the crowd, which had already come out from between the fences. Figures pass; caps and helmets fly from the heads. A golden dust rises on the road, for the day is dry and sunny. On both sides of the way the ripening grain rustles with heavy head, and bends under the light breeze, which blows mildly from time to time. In the blue sky the larks are soaring and singing as if they had gone mad.

The station! The crowds are still greater. At the station are men summoned from Upper Kryvda, Lower Kryvda, from Vyvlashchyntse, from Nyedolya, from Mizerov. Movement, noise, disorder! The walls of the station are covered with proclamations. War is present, "in the name of God and the Fatherland." The *Landwehr* will go to protect their native homes, their wives, their children, their cottages, and fields. The French, it is clear, hold in special hatred Pognembin, Upper Kryvda, Lower Kryvda, Vyvlashchyntse, Nyedolya, and

Mizerov. It seems so at least to those who read the proclamations. New crowds are coming continually to the front of the station. In the hall the smoke of pipes fills the air and hides the proclamations. In the uproar it is difficult for people to understand one another; everything is moving, shouting, screaming. On the platform are heard German commands, the strong words of which have a brief, firm, peremptory sound.

A bell is heard, a whistle! from a distance comes the violent breath of the engine, — every moment nearer, clearer. It seems to be the war itself approaching in person.

A second bell. A quiver runs through every breast. Some woman begins to scream, "Yadom, Yadom!" She is calling evidently her Adam. But other women catch up the expression, and cry, "Yadan, Yadan!" (they are coming). Some voice more shrill than others adds, "Frantsuzy yadan!" (the French are coming!) and in the twinkle of an eye a panic seizes not only the women but the future heroes of Sedan. The crowd is stirred up. Meanwhile the train has stopped at the station. In all the windows are visible uniforms, and caps with red bands. The troops are apparently as numerous as ants. In coal-cars the sullen, long-bodied cannon seem black ; on platform-cars a forest of bayonets is bristling. Evidently the command has been given to the soldiers to sing, for the whole train is just quivering from the strong voices of men. A certain power and might is beating from that train, the end of which is not to be seen.

On the platform they are beginning to marshal the recruits ; whoever has the chance takes farewell once more. Bartek, waving his paws like the wings of a wind-mill, thrusts out his eyes.

"Now, Magda, farewell ! "

"Oi, my poor fellow ! "

"Thou wilt see me no more ! "

"I shall see thee no more ! "

"There is no help of any kind!"

"May the Mother of God guard thee and save thee!"

"Farewell! keep the cottage."

The woman caught him by the neck, with weeping.

"May God go with thee."

The last moment has come. The whining, weeping, and lamenting of women drown for some moments everything. "Farewell! Farewell!" But now the soldiers are separated from the crowd; they are already a dark, dense mass which forms into squares and rectangles, and begins to move with the regularity and precision of a machine. The command comes, "Seats!" The squares and rectangles break in the centre, move toward the cars in narrow lines, and vanish inside them. In the distance the engine whistles, and puffs forth rolls of blue smoke. Now it pants like a dragon, and ejects streams of vapor. The lamentation of women reaches the highest pitch. Some cover

their eyes with their aprons; others stretch
their hands toward the cars. With sobbing
voices they repeat the names of their husbands
and sons.

"Farewell, Bartek!" cries Magda from below; "and go not where thou 'rt not sent.
May the Mother of God — Farewell! O God
help us!"

"But take care of the cottage!" calls Bartek.

The line quivers suddenly; the cars strike
one another, and move.

"But remember that thou hast a wife and a
child!" screams Magda, running after the train.
"Farewell, in the name of the Father, Son, and
Holy Ghost! Farewell!"

The train moves with increasing rapidity,
bearing warriors from Pognembin, from both
Kryvdas, from Nyedolya, and Mizerov.

II.

ON one side, Magda is returning to Pognembin with a crowd of women, and
crying; on the other, the train is rushing forth
into the blue distance, bristling with bayonets,
and on it is Bartek. The end of the blue distance is not to be seen. Pognembin, too, is
barely visible. Only the poplars stand looking
gray, and the church-tower shines in gold, for
the sun is playing on it. Soon the poplars
have vanished, and the golden cross seems
merely a shining point. While that point was
shining, Bartek gazed at it; but when it vanished also, there was no end to the sorrow of
the man. A great faintness seized him, and he
felt that he was lost. He began then to look
at the corporal, for besides God there was
no one else above him. What will happen to

him now? The corporal's head is there to
answer that question. Bartek himself knows
nothing, understands nothing. The corporal
sits on a bench, holds his musket, and smokes
a pipe. The smoke, as if a cloud, shades every
little while his serious and anxious face. Not
Bartek's eyes alone are looking on that face;
all eyes are looking on it from every corner of
the car. In Pognembin or Kryvda every Bartek
or Voitek is his own master; each must think
of himself for himself; but now the corporal
is there for that purpose. If he commands
them to look toward the right, they look
toward the right; if he commands them to look
toward the left, they look toward the left.
Each one asks him with a glance, " Well, what
will happen to us? " and he himself knows as
much as they, and would be glad also if a
superior were to give him in this regard some
command or explanation. Besides, the men
are afraid to ask in words, for it is war time,
with the complete apparatus of courts-martial.

What is permitted and what is not permitted is
unknown, — at least to them; and they are
alarmed by the sound of expressions such as
" Kriegsgericht " (court-martial), which they
do not understand well, but fear all the more.

At the same time they feel that this corporal
is more necessary to them now than at the
manœuvres near Poznan, for he alone knows
everything, — he thinks for them; and without
him not a stir. Meanwhile the musket has
grown burdensome to the corporal, for he
throws it to Bartck to hold. Bartek seizes the
gun hurriedly, holds his breath, stares and
looks at the corporal as at a rainbow; but
there is little comfort to him from that.

Oi ! there must be bad news, for the corporal
looks as if taken from a cross. At the stations
there are songs and shouting; the corporal
commands, hurries about, scolds, so as to exhibit himself to his superiors; but when the
train moves, all are silent, and he is silent.
For him, too, the world has two sides at

present, one clear and understandable, — that
is his cottage, his wife, and the feather-bed;
the other, dark, perfectly dark, — that is France
and the war.   His ardor, like the ardor of the
whole army, would be glad to borrow its gait
from the crab.   Their courage roused the warriors of Pognembin the more evidently that it
was sitting not in them, but on the shoulder of
each man.   And since every soldier carried on
his back a knapsack, a cloak, and other military
belongings, the weight was too much for each
man of them.

Meanwhile the train snorted, roared, and flew
into the distance.   At every station new cars
and engines were attached.   At every station
were to be seen only helmets, cannon, horses,
the bayonets of infantry, and the flags of Ulans.
A clear evening came down gradually.   The
sun lost its rays in a purple twilight; high in the
heavens droves of small light clouds were moving with edges darkened by the sunset.   The
train ceased at last to take people at the sta-

tions; it only rattled, and flew farther into that redness as into a sea of blood. From the open car in which Bartek was sitting with the men of Pognembin, were to be seen villages, settlements, and towns, the towers on the churches, storks bent like hooks, standing on one leg at their nests, single cottages, cherry-gardens, — all gleamed in passing, and all were red. The soldiers began to whisper to one another, the more boldly that the corporal, having put his knapsack under his head, had fallen asleep, with his porcelain pipe between his teeth. Voitek Gvizdala, a man from Pognembin, sitting next to Bartek, pushed him with his elbow, —

"Bartek, but listen!"

Bartek turned his face toward him, with anxious staring eyes.

"Why look like a calf going to the slaughter?" whispered Voitek; "and thou, poor fellow, art going surely to the slaughter."

"Oi, oi!" groaned Bartek.

" Art afraid ? " asked Voitek.

" Why should I not be afraid ? "

The twilight had become ruddier. Voitek stretched his hand toward it, and whispered on, —

" Seest thou that brightness? Know'st, stupid fellow, what that is? That is blood. This is Poland, our country. Dost understand? But there, far away where it shines so, that is France."

" But shall we get there soon ? "

" Art in a hurry? They say 't is terribly far away. But never fear : the French will come to meet us."

Bartek began to work heavily with his Pognembin head ; after a while he asked, —

" Voitek ! "

" What ? "

" Well, for example, what kind of people are the French ? "

Here Voitek's learning saw on a sudden in front of it an abyss into which it might plunge head-foremost more easily than fly back again. He knew that the French are Frenchmen. He had heard something about them from older men, who said that they always conquered everybody; finally, he knew that they are some kind of very foreign people; but how was he to explain this to Bartek so that he might know how foreign they are. First of all he repeated the question, —

" What kind of people are they? "

" That 's it."

Three nations were known to Voitek : in the middle were the Poles; on one side the " Moskale " (Muscovites) ; on the other, the Germans, — but various kinds of Germans. Preferring to be clear rather than accurate, he said, —

" What kind of people are the French? How can I tell thee? they are just such Germans, only still worse."

And Bartek in answer to that : " Oh, the carrion ! "

Hitherto he had had only one feeling touching the French, — a feeling of indescribable
fear; now that Prussian *Landwehrmann* began
to feel toward them a rather distinct patriotic
dislike. Still he did not understand it all
clearly yet; hence he inquired again, —

"But will Germans fight against Germans?"

Here Voitek, like a second Socrates, determined to proceed by the method of comparison,
and answered, —

"But does not thy Lysek fight with my
Burek?"

Bartek opened his mouth, and looked awhile
at his master, —

"Oh, that is true."

"Besides, the Austrians are Germans," said
Voitek; "and have not our people fought with
them? Old Svesrshch said that when he was at
the war, Steinmetz shouted to them, 'Forward,
boys, against the Germans!' But it won't be
so easy with the French!"

"Oh. for God's sake!"

"The French have never lost a war. The man that they get hold of can never get away, never fear. Every man of them is equal to two or three on our side ; and they have beards like Jews. Sometimes they are as black as the Devil. At sight of such people commit thyself to God."

"Well, but why do we go against them?" asked Bartek, in desperation.

That philosophic question was not so stupid as it seemed to Voitek, who, under the evident influence of official inspiration, hastened with an answer, —

"They have a most bitter hatred of our men. People say that they are so hungry for the land here because they want to smuggle *vodka* out of the kingdom, and the Government will not let them ; and that's the cause of the war. Well, dost understand?"

"Why should n't I understand?" said Bartek, with resignation.

Voitek continued, "And they are as greedy for women as a dog for cheese."

"In that case they would n't let Magda pass?"

"They would n't let even old women pass."

"Oh!" cried Bartek, in such a tone as if he wished to say, "If that is true I 'll fight!"

And, in fact, it seemed to him that that was too much. Let them smuggle *vodka*, if they like, from the kingdom; but let them keep away from Magda. Now my Bartek began to look on the whole war from the point of view of his own interest, and to feel a certain consolation in the thought that so many troops and cannon were moving forward to defend Magda, who was threatened by the seductions of the French. His fists were clinched involuntarily, and fear of the French was mingled in his mind with hatred of them. He came to the conviction that there was no escape; it was necessary to go.

Meanwhile the brightness of the sky had vanished. It was dark. The car, moving on rails of unequal elevation, began to sway powerfully, and, in keeping with its motion, the helmets and bayonets nodded to the left and right.

One hour passed, and a second. From the engine were showered millions of sparks, which crossed one another in the darkness like long golden streaks and small serpents. Bartek was not able to sleep for a long time. As those sparks shot through the air, so did thoughts in his mind touching the war, Magda, Pognembin, the French, and the Germans. It seemed to him that even had he wished he could not raise himself from the bench on which he was sitting. He fell asleep; but with an unwholesome half-sleep. Immediately visions flew to him; he saw first of all his Lysek fighting his neighbor's Burek, till the dogs' hearts were flying in them. He grasps after his stick to stop them, but sees all at once something else: at Magda's side a Frenchman is sitting, black as the holy earth; and the satisfied Magda is laughing, and showing her teeth.

Other Frenchmen are sneering at Bartek, and pointing at him with their fingers. Of course it is the engine puffing; but it seems to him the Frenchmen are calling, "Magda! Magda! Magda!" Bartek screams, "Shut your snouts, you scoundrels! let the woman go!" But they cry, "Magda! Magda! Magda!" Lysek and Burek are barking; all Pognembin is shouting, "Don't give up the woman!" Is Bartek tied, or what? He struggles, pulls, his fetters break. Bartek seizes the Frenchmen by the head, and all at once —

All at once he is shaken by a violent pain as from a heavy blow. Bartek wakes and springs to his feet. The whole car is roused. All ask what has happened. But poor Bartek has caught the corporal by the beard. Now he is standing erect as a post, two fingers at his temple, and the officer is waving his hand, and shouting as if mad, —

"Ach Sie! Dummes Vieh aus der Polakei! Hau' ich den Lümmel in die Fresse. das ihm

die Zähne sektionenweise aus dem Maule
herausfliegen werden! [Oh, stupid beast from
Poland! I will whack the clown in the snout
so the teeth will fly out of his mouth in
sections!] "

The corporal is hoarse from rage; but Bartek
stands unmoved, with his fingers at his temple.
The soldiers are biting their lips so as not to
laugh; but they are afraid, for out of the corporal's mouth are falling yet the last arrows:
" Ein polnischer Ochse! Ochse aus Podolien!
(Polish ox, ox from Podolia!) "

At last everything is quiet. Bartek sits down
on his old place again. He feels that his
cheeks begin to tingle somehow, and the
engine as if in spite repeats continually:

" Magda! Magda! Magda! "

He felt also some kind of great sorrow.

III.

MORNING! A scattered pale light shines on faces which are sleepy and weary from lack of rest. The soldiers are sleeping on the bench, without order; some with their heads on their breasts, others with their heads dropped back. The morning comes, and fills the whole world with rosy light. It is fresh and wholesome. The soldiers wake up. The bright morning brings out of shadow and mist a certain country to them unknown. Hei! but where now is Pognembin, where Upper and Lower Kryvda, where Mizerov? Here it is strange, and everything is different. The high land round about is shaded with oaks; in the valleys the houses are covered with red roofs, with black milkwort on the walls, — houses beautiful as palaces, grown around with grape-vines.

Here and there are churches with pointed towers, here and there mill chimneys with plumes
of rosy smoke. But somehow, it is crowded;
there is a lack of grain-fields. The people are
numerous as ants. Villages and towns shoot
by. The train, without stopping, passes a
number of smaller stations. Something must
have happened, for everywhere crowds are to
be seen. The sun comes up slowly from behind the hills; therefore, one and another
Matsek begin their " Our Father " aloud.
Others follow their example. The first rays
put their glitter on the prayerful and serious
faces of the men.

Meanwhile the train stops at the main
station. A throng of people surrounds it at
once. News from the seat of war, a victory !
a victory ! The despatches had come some
hours before. All were expecting defeat, and
when news of success waked them, their joy
knew no bounds. People half dressed left
their beds and hurried to the station. From

some roofs flags are waving already, and in
all hands are handkerchiefs. They bring beer
to the cars, tobacco, and cigars. The enthusiasm is beyond description, faces are radiant.
"Die Wacht am Rhein" is roaring like a storm.
Some are weeping, others fall into one another's
embraces. "*Unser Fritz* has crushed them to
pieces! cannon and flags are captured!" With
noble enthusiasm the crowd give the soldiers
everything they have. Joy enters the hearts
of the soldiers, and they begin to sing too.
The cars are trembling from the deep voices
of the men, and the crowds listen with wonder to the words of songs which they understand not. The Pognembin men are singing,
"Bartosh! Bartosh! O lose not thy hope."
"Die Polen! Die Polen!" repeat the crowd
by way of explanation, and gather around the
cars, wondering at the appearance of the soldiers, and at the same time strengthening
themselves by relating anecdotes of the terrible bravery of those Polish regiments.

Bartek has swollen cheeks, which with his yellow mustaches, staring eyes, and enormous bony form make him terrible. They look on him as a special beast. What defenders the Germans have! He will fix the French! Bartek smiles with satisfaction, for he too is glad that they have beaten the French, who at least will not come to Pognembin to lead Magda astray; they won't take his land. He smiles then; but since his face pains him greatly, he twists it withal, and in truth he is terrible. But he eats with the appetite of an Homeric hero; pea-sausage and goblets of beer vanish in his mouth as in a cavern. They give him cigars, *pfennigs;* he takes everything.

"They are a good kind of people, these German fellows," says he to Voitek; but after a while he adds, "But seest thou they have beaten the French?"

The sceptical Voitek casts a shadow on his joy. Voitek is a Cassandra-like prophet.

"The French always let themselves be

beaten in the beginning so as to lead men astray, but afterward when they go at it the chips fly."

Voitek did not know that the greater part of Europe shared his opinion; and still less did he know that all Europe was mistaken together with him.

They went farther. Every house within eyesight was covered with flags. At some stations they were detained longer, for every place was filled with trains. Troops were hastening from all parts of Germany to strengthen their victorious brethren. The trains were adorned with green crowns. The Ulans held on their lances bouquets of flowers, given them on the road. Among the Ulans the majority were Poles also. Cries were heard often from the cars, —

"How are ye, boys? and whither is God leading you?"

Sometimes from a train flying past on a neighboring track came the well-known song:

> "From the other side of Sandomir
> The maiden calls her soldier — "

And then Bartek and his comrades catch up :

"Oh, soldier, come and love me.
I have not eaten yet — May God reward thee !"

In the same degree in which all had left
Pognembin in sorrow were they now full of
spirit and enthusiasm. The first train with the
first wounded coming from France destroyed
that good feeling, however. The train with
the wounded halts at Deutz, and halts long
to let those pass who are hastening to the
field of combat. But before all can pass the
bridge at Cologne some hours are consumed.
Bartek rushes with others to look at the sick
and wounded. Some are lying in covered cars,
others for want of room in open ones, and the
latter could be seen easily. At the first glance
the heroic courage of Bartek flew out again to
his shoulder.

"Come here, Voitek," cried he with terror ;
"but see how many men these French have
spoiled !" And there is something to look

at ! — pale suffering faces, some black from powder or pain, bespattered with blood. In answer to the general rejoicing these give only groans. Some of them curse the war of French against Germans. Parched and dry lips cry every moment for water; eyes gaze as in madness. Here and there among the wounded is to be seen the stiffened face of one dying, — sometimes calm, with blue around the eyes, sometimes distorted from convulsions, with wild stare and grinning teeth. Bartek sees for the first time the bloody fruits of war. A new chaos rises in his head; he looks like a stunned man, and stands in the throng with mouth open; they knock against him on every side; a policeman pushes him with the but of his musket in the shoulder. He seeks Voitek with his eyes, finds him, and says, —

"Voitek, God save us! oh!"

"It will be that way with thee, too."

"Jesus Mary! And so people kill each other like that! Why, when a man in a village strikes another the police take him to the court and punish him."

"That may be; but now the best man is he who kills most people. Didst think, stupid fellow, that thou wouldst fire off powder as at the manœuvres or at a mark, — not at men?"

Here, there was an evident difference between theory and practice. Our Bartek was a soldier however. He had been at manœuvres and musters, had fired guns, and knew that war was for men to kill one another; but now when he saw the blood of the wounded, the misery of war, he felt so sick and faint that he could hardly stand on his feet. He gained new respect for the French, which decreased only when he crossed from Deutz to Cologne. At the central station he saw prisoners for the first time. They were surrounded by a multitude of soldiers, and by people who looked at them with feelings of importance, but still without hatred. Bartek pressed through the crowd, pushing people aside with his elbow; he looked at the car and was astonished.

The crowd of French infantry in torn cloaks, small, dirty, suffering, filled the car as closely as herrings fill a cask. Many of them stretched out their hands for the scant gifts which the crowd bestowed on them so far as the guards did not prevent. Bartek, according to what he had heard from Voitek, had an altogether different picture in his mind of the French. Courage returned from his shoulder to his breast again. He looked around for Voitek. Voitek was at his side.

"What didst thou tell me?" asked Bartek. "They are poor little fellows. If I should knock the head off one of them the life would go out of three others."

"They must have wasted away somehow," said Voitek, equally disenchanted.

"In what language are they chattering?"

"Be sure 't is not Polish."

Satisfied in this regard Bartek went farther along the cars.

"Miserable fellows!" said he, finishing his review of the soldiers of the line.

But in the next cars sat Zouaves. These gave Bartek more to think of. Since they sat in covered cars it was impossible to determine whether each was as big as two or three common men; but through the windows could be seen the long beards and warlike, serious faces of old soldiers with dark complexions, and eyes gleaming terribly. Bartek's courage went again to his shoulder.

"Those are more dangerous," whispered he, as if fearing that they might hear him.

"Thou hast not seen those yet who would not let themselves be taken," said Voitek.

"God guard us!"

"Thou wilt see them!"

When they had looked at the Zouaves, they went farther. At the next car Bartek sprang back as if burned.

"Oh, rescue! Voitek, save me!"

In the open window was visible the dark,

almost black, face of a Turko, with the whites of his eyes turned out. He must have been wounded, for his face was distorted from suffering.

" What is that?" asked Voitek.

" That is the Evil One, not a soldier. God be merciful to me a sinner ! "

" But look at him ; what teeth he has ! "

" Oh, devil take him ! I will not look at him."

Bartek was silent, but after a while he asked, —

" Voitek ! "

" What? "

" If such a one were christened, would n't it help? "

" Pagans have no understanding of the holy faith."

The order was given to take seats. After a while the train moved. When it grew dark, Bartek saw before him continually the black face of the Turko and the terrible whites of his eyes. From the feelings which at that moment possessed this warrior of Pognembin, it was not possible to prophesy much concerning his future exploits.

IV.

A N intimate part in the general engagement at Gravelotte convinced Bartek at first of this only, — that in a battle there is something to stare at, but nothing to do. To begin with, he and his regiment were commanded to stand with grounded arms at the foot of a hill covered with grape-vines. From a distance cannon are playing; near by cavalry regiments are flying past with a thunder from which the ground trembles; now flaglets are glittering, now the swords of cuirassiers. On the hill through the blue sky grenades fly hissing in the form of white cloudlets; smoke fills the air. and hides the horizon. It seems that the battle, like a storm, will go past at the sides; but doubt does not last long.

After a time certain wonderful movements rise around Bartek's regiment. Other regiments begin to take their places near it; and in the interval between them cannons are swept in with all horse-speed, unlimbered in a flash, and their jaws turned toward the hill-top. The whole valley is filled with troops. Every place is thundering with commands; adjutants are flying. But our men in the ranks are whispering one to another, "Oi, we shall catch it, we shall!" or they ask one another with alarm, "Is it beginning?" — "Surely it is." Now comes uncertainty, a riddle, — maybe death. In the smoke which covers the hill-top something is seething and rattling terribly. Nearer and nearer are heard the deep roar of cannon and the rattling of musketry-fire. From a distance comes, as it were, some undefined crashing; those are the *mitrailleuses*. Suddenly, when the newly-placed cannon roar,

the earth and the air tremble together. Before
Bartek's regiment there is a terrible hissing.
They look : something is flying bright as a
rose, like a cloudlet, and in that cloudlet
something is hissing, laughing, gnashing its
teeth, neighing, and howling. The men cry,
" Grenade ! grenade ! " Then that bird of
war, moving like a whirlwind, approaches, falls,
bursts ! A dreadful roar tears the ears, — an
outburst as if the world were falling, and a
blow as if from a wind-stroke. Disorder in the
ranks standing near the cannon, a cry, and a
command, " Attention ! " Bartek stands in the
first rank, his gun at his shoulder, his head
erect, his beard motionless ; therefore his teeth
are not chattering. It is not permitted to
tremble, it is not permitted to fire. Stand !
Wait ! The second grenade comes, the third,
the fourth, the tenth ! The wind blows the
smoke away from the hill. The French have
driven from it the Prussian batteries, have
placed there their own, which are now vomit-

ing fire into the valley. Every moment long
white darts of smoke are shooting out of the
vineyard. The infantry, under cover of the
cannon, are descending lower and lower, so as
to open a musketry-fire. Now they are perfectly visible; for the wind has borne away
the smoke. Has the vineyard bloomed with
poppies? No, those are the red caps of infantry. At once they disappear among the tall
grape-vines; they are not to be seen, — only
here and there a tri-colored flag. The musketry-fire begins, — quick, feverish, irregular;
bursts forth suddenly every moment in new
places. Above that fire, howling continually,
come the grenades, and cross one another in
the air. On the hill shouts burst forth, which
are answered in the valley by German hurrahs.
Cannon from the valley roar uninterruptedly.
The regiment stands immovable.

The circle of fire begins, however, to enclose
it from the flanks. The bullets from afar buzz
like horse-flies or shoot past with a terrible

whistle. Every moment there are more of them, — now they are whistling around the heads, noses, eyes, shoulders of the men; thousands of them are coming, millions. It is a marvel that a man is left standing yet. All at once behind Bartek is heard a groan, "Jesus!" then "Close!" again "Jesus!" "Close!" At last there is one unbroken groan; the commands come more quickly; the ranks close; the whistling is more frequent; then unceasing and awful. The slain are dragged out by the feet. The judgment of God is there present.

"Art afraid?" asks Voitek.

"Why should n't I be?" answers our hero, with chattering teeth.

And both stand there, Bartek and Voitek, and it does n't even come into their heads that it is possible to run. They were ordered to stand; and that is the end of it! Bartek did not tell the truth. He was not so much afraid as thousands of others would have been in his place.   Discipline lorded it over his imagination, and his imagination did not paint to him the situation in its dreadful reality.   Still Bartek thought that they would kill him, and he conveyed that thought to Voitek.

"There will be no hole in heaven if such a fool is killed," answered Voitek, with vexation.

These words pacify Bartek considerably. It seems to him that the main question for him is whether there will be a hole in heaven.   Pacified in this regard, he stands patiently; only feels terribly hot, and the sweat streams over his face.   Meanwhile the fire becomes so murderous that the ranks are melting before their eyes.   There is no one to drag away the killed and the wounded; the groans of the dying are mingled with the whistling of missiles and the roar of musketry.   By the movement of the tri-colored flag it is clear that the infantry concealed in the vineyard are coming nearer and nearer.   The crowds of *mitrail-*

leuses are decimating the ranks, which despair is now seizing.

But in the sounds of that despair is felt the muttering of impatience and rage. If they are commanded to advance they will go like a storm. Only they cannot stand in one place. Some soldier tears his cap from his head on a sudden, hurls it with all force to the ground, and says, —

"One death to the goat!"

Bartek found again a known consolation in these words, so that he ceased almost to fear. For if death must come once, it is no great question. That peasant philosophy is better than any other, since it gives consolation. Bartek knew before, of course, that death must come once; but it was pleasant for him to hear this, and to have complete certainty, especially since the battle had begun to turn into utter defeat. Think of it, — that regiment, without firing a shot, is already half annihilated! Crowds of soldiers from other scattered regiments are rushing past in disorder; but these men from Pognembin, from Upper and Lower Kryvda and Mizerov, held by the iron discipline of Prussia, are standing still. But in their ranks a certain hesitation is felt. In a moment the bonds of discipline will burst. The ground under their feet is growing soft and slippery from blood, the raw smell of which is mixed with the smell of the powder-smoke. In certain places the ranks cannot close, for corpses block the way. At the feet of those men who are still standing, the other half of the regiment is lying in blood, in groans, in convulsions, dying or in the grasp of death. Air fails the breath. A murmur is rising in the ranks, —

"They have brought us here to be slaughtered !"

"No one will go from this place."

"Still, Polnishes Vieh !" sounds the voice of an officer.

"It is well for you behind my collar !"

"Steht der Kerl da!"

Suddenly some voice begins to speak, —

"Under Thy protection —"

Bartek accompanies at once, "We take refuge, Holy Mother of God!"

And soon a chorus of Polish voices is calling out on that field of destruction to the Patroness of Chenstohova, "Reject not our prayers!" And from under their feet groans accompany them, "O Mary, O Mary!" And she heard them evidently, for that moment an adjutant rushes up on a foaming horse. "To the attack! Hurrah! Forward!"

The ridge of bayonets is lowered suddenly; the rank stretches in a long line, and rushes toward the hill, seeking with the bayonet those enemies which it could not find with the eye. But from the foot of the hill our men are divided yet by two hundred yards, and this distance must be crossed under a murderous fire. Will they not be slaughtered to the last man, or will they not run? They may be

exterminated; but they will not draw back, for
the Prussian commander knows what note to
play for the attack. Amid the bellowing of
cannon, amid musketry-fire, smoke, confusion,
and groans, louder than all the trumpets and
drums is rising to heaven the hymn at which
every drop of blood dances in their bosoms.
" Poland is not lost ! " Hurrah ! " While we
are living ! " answer the Poles. Enthusiasm
seizes them; a flame is beating in their faces.
They go like a storm over prostrate bodies of
men and horses, over fragments of cannon.
They perish, but sweep forward with shouting
and singing. They have reached already the
edge of the vineyard. They vanish among
the vines; but the hymn rises. At once their
bayonets are gleaming. On the hill the fire is
seething still more terribly. In the valley the
trumpets are playing continually. The French
discharges become quicker and quicker, feverish, and on a sudden are silent.

Down in the valley Steinmetz — that old wolf

of war — lights a porcelain pipe, and speaks in tones of satisfaction, —

"Only give them that music ! They have got there, bold fellows ! " In fact, the next instant one of the tri-colored standards waving proudly springs up, stoops, and vanishes.

"They are not joking ! " said Steinmetz.

The trumpets play the same hymn again. Another Poznan regiment rushes on to help the first. In the thicket a battle with bayonets rages up.

O Muse ! sing now, my Bartek, that posterity may know what he did ! In his heart fear, terror, impatience, despair, were blended in the single feeling of rage ; and when he heard that music, every nerve in him was as rigid as steel wire. His hair was on end ; sparks flew from his eyes. He forgot the world, — forgot that death must come once ; and seizing in his mighty paws the musket, ran on with the others. When he had run to the hill, he fell to the ground at least ten times, bruised his nose, covered himself with earth and with the blood which was running from his nose, and hurried forward, mad, panting, catching the air with open mouth. He was staring his eyes out to see in the thicket at the soonest some Frenchman; and at last he saw three at once at a standard. They were Turkos. But do you think that Bartek drew back? No! he would have taken Lucifer himself by the horns at that moment. He rushed at the three men, and they with a howl rushed at him; two bayonets, like two stings, are already touching his breast; but my Bartek takes his musket like a club by the small end, whirls it, strikes. A terrible cry answers him, a groan, — and two black bodies are quivering on the ground.

That moment about ten comrades ran with assistance to the third, who was holding a flag. Bartek sprang like a fury on all at once. They fired; there was a flash and a report, and at the same time in the rolls of smoke thundered the hoarse bellow of Bartek. —

" Ye have missed ! "

And again the musket in his hand described a terrible half-circle; again groans answered his blows. The Turkos drew back in terror at sight of this giant, wild with rage; and whether Bartek heard wrongly, or they cried out something in Arabic, 't is enough that it seemed to him distinctly that from their broad lips came the cry, —

" Magda ! Magda ! "

" Ye want Magda ! " howled Bartek, and with one spring he was in the midst of the enemy.

Happily a number of Matseks and Voiteks and other Barteks hurried up in that moment to aid him. In the midst of the thicket of vines a battle sprang up, hand to hand, close, which was accompanied by the crash of muskets, the whistling of nostrils, and the feverish puffing of the combatants. Bartek raged like a storm. Scorched with smoke, covered with blood, more like a beast than a man, caring for

nothing, — he overturned men with every blow,
broke muskets, smashed heads.   His hands
moved with the terrible swiftness of a machine
scattering destruction.   He rushed to the standard-bearer, seized him with iron fingers by
the throat.   The eyes of the standard-bearer
were bursting from his head, his face was blue,
he coughed, and his hands dropped the staff.

"Hurrah!" cried Bartek; and raising the
flag, he waved it in the air.

General Steinmetz saw from the valley that
rising and falling standard; but he could see
it only during one twinkle of an eye, for in the
next twinkle Bartek, with that same standard,
crushed in some head covered with a cap in
gold lace.

Meanwhile his comrades had rushed ahead;
Bartek was left for one instant alone.   He
tore off the flag, hid it in his bosom, and, seizing the staff with both hands, hurried after his
comrades.   Crowds of Turkos, howling with
unhuman voices, rushed to the cannon standing

on the summit of the hill; after them rushed the Poles, shouting, chasing, crushing them with gun-stocks, and stabbing with bayonets.

The Zouaves, standing at the guns, greeted pursuers and pursued with musketry-fire.

" Hurrah ! " cried Bartek.

The Poles rushed to the cannon. A new battle rose up, hand to hand. At this moment the second Pognembin regiment came up to support the first. The flag-staff in Bartek's powerful paws was turned this time into a kind of infernal flail. Every blow of it opened a free road in the dense ranks of the Frenchmen. Fear began to seize the Zouaves and the Turkos. In the place where Bartek was fighting they fled. Bartek was the first to sit on a cannon, as he would on his Pognembin mare.

But before the soldiers had time to see him there he was sitting on a second one, where he overturned the flag-bearer with his flag.

" Hurrah, Bartek ! " repeated the soldiers.

The victory was complete. All the *mitral-*

leuses were captured. The fleeing infantry came upon a new Prussian regiment on the other side of the hill, and laid down their arms.

Bartek in the pursuit captured a third flag. It was necessary to see him when, wearied, covered with sweat and blood, puffing like a blacksmith's bellows, he came down with the others from the hill, bearing on his shoulders three flags. The Frenchmen! hei! what had he done with them? At his side walked the torn and slashed Voitek. Bartek said to him:

"What didst thou say to me? They are only worms, there is no strength in their bones. They scratched me and thee like cats, but that is all; and when I struck a man he went to the ground."

"Who knew that thou wert so venomous?" answered Voitek, who had seen Bartek's deeds, and began to look at him now with different eyes altogether.

But who had not seen those deeds? History,

the whole regiment, most of the officers, — all looked now with wonder on that gigantic fellow with his thin yellow mustaches and staring eyes.

"Ach! Sie verfluchter Polake (eh! you cursed Pole)!" said the major himself, and took him by the ear. And Bartek showed his back teeth with delight. When the regiment stood in line again at the foot of the hill, the major pointed him out to the colonel and the colonel to Steinmetz himself.

Steinmetz looked at the flags and gave command to take them; then he began to look at Bartek. My Bartek stretches out like a string again and presents arms; but the old general looks at him and shakes his head with satisfaction. At last he begins to say something to the colonel. The word *Unter-officier* (Underofficer) was heard distinctly.

"Zu dumm, Excellenz (too stupid, your Excellency)," answered the major.

"Let us try," said his Excellency, and turning his horse approached Bartek.

Bartek himself knew not what was coming to him, — a thing unheard of in the Prussian army: a general will speak with a soldier! His Excellency will do that the more easily since he knows Polish. Besides, that soldier had captured three flags and two cannon.

"From what place art thou?" asked the general.

"From Pognembin," answered Bartek.

"Well.   And thy name?"

"Bartek Slovik."

"Mensch (man)," explained the major, who stood behind his Excellency.

"*Mens!*" repeated Bartek.

"Knowst why thou art beating the French?"

"I know, Tselentsiyo."

"Tell me."

Bartek began to stutter: "For — for—"

On a sudden the words of Voitek came by good luck to his memory; he blurted them out quickly so as not to misplace them, —

"Because they are Germans too, — only worse, the carrion!"

The face of the old Excellency began to
quiver as if he were about to burst into
laughter. After a moment however he turned
to the major and said, —

"You were right."

My Bartek, self satisfied, stood straight as a
string.

"Who won the battle to-day?" asked the
general again.

"I, Tselentsiyo," answered Bartek, without
hesitation.

The face of the general began to quiver again.

"True, true; and here is thy reward."

The old warrior unfastened the iron cross
from his own breast, then bent and fastened it
to Bartek. The good-humor of the general in
a perfectly natural way was reflected on the
faces of the colonel, the majors, the captains,
and down to the corporals. When the general
was gone, the colonel on his part gave ten
thalers to Bartek, the major five, and so on.
All repeat to him, laughing, that he had won

the battle. In consequence of this Bartek was in the seventh heaven.

A wonderful thing, Voitek was the only man not very much pleased with our hero !

In the evening when they had taken their places at the fire and the noble countenance of Bartek was stuffed with pea-sausage as tightly as the sausage itself was stuffed with peas, Voitek called out with a tone of resignation, —

" Oh, thou, Bartek, art stupid, oh, stupid ! "

"But why?" asked Bartek, through his sausage.

" Why, man, didst thou tell the general that the French were Germans?"

" But thou didst say so thyself."

" But thou shouldst know that the general and officers are Germans themselves."

" But what of that?"

Voitek began somehow to stutter something, — " Though they are Germans that is not to be said to them. for it is awkward."

" But I said that about the French, not about them."

" Ei, even if thou didst, still — "

Voitek stopped suddenly. Clearly he wished himself too to say something else, — he wished to explain to Bartek that in presence of the German it was not right to speak ill of Germans ; but somehow his tongue became twisted.

V.

SOMETIME after, the Royal Prussian mail brought to Pognembin the following letter : —

MOST BELOVED MAGDA, — May Jesus Christ be praised and His Holy Mother! What is to be heard at home? It is well for thee in the cottage under the feathers, and I here fighting terribly. We were around the great fortress of Metz, and I so pounded the French that all the cavalry and infantry were astonished; and the general himself was astonished and said that I won the battle, and he gave me a cross. Now the officers and under-

14

officers respect me greatly, and do not beat me on the snout much. After that we marched on, and there was a second battle; but I have forgotten how the place is called; and I fought also and took a fourth flag, and the greatest colonel of cuirassiers I seized and took captive. The under-officer advises me to write a petition and ask to be left here when our regiments are sent home. In war there is no place to sleep, but all a man can hold to eat; and there is wine in this country everywhere, for the people are rich. When we burned a village we did n't spare the children or women, and I did like the rest. A church was burned to the ground, for the French are Catholics, and not a few people were burned. We are going now against the Kaiser himself, and there will be an end of the war; but do thou take care of the cottage and Franek. If not, when I come home I 'll so fix thee that thou wilt not know who I am. I commit thee to God.

BARTEK SLOVIK.

Bartek had got a taste for war, evidently, and began to look at it as his own special craft. He had gained great confidence in himself, and went now to battle as if to some work in

Pognembin. After every engagement medals and crosses flew to his breast; and though he was not made an under-officer, he was held by all to be the first soldier in the regiment. He was always obedient as before, and possessed the blind bravery of a man who cannot estimate danger. His valor did not come now, as in the first moments, from rage. The source of it now was military practice, and faith in himself. Besides, his gigantic strength endured all hardships, marching and watching. Men perished around him, — he alone endured without exhaustion; only he grew fiercer, and became more and more a stern Prussian man-at-arms. He began not only to beat the French, but to hate them. His other ideas also were changed. He became a soldier-patriot, and worshipped blindly his leaders. In the next letter he wrote to Magda : —

Voitek was torn into two pieces ; but such is war, thou knowest. Besides, he was a fool, for he said that the French were Germans, while they are French, and the Germans are our people."

Magda in answer to both letters railed at him as follows : —

MOST BELOVED BARTEK, — We were married before the holy altar! May God punish thee! Thou art a fool thyself, Pagan, for in company with Chestnuts thou art murdering a Catholic people. Thou dost not understand that the Chestnuts are Lutherans, and thou, a Catholic, art helping them. Thou wish'st war, lazy-bones, for thou canst do nothing but fight and drink and kill people, and not observe fasts but burn churches. God knows that thou 'lt be burned in hell if thou boast of thy deeds, and hast pity neither for old people nor children. Remember, sheep, what is written for the Polish people in the holy faith with golden letters from the beginning of the world to the last day of judgment when the Highest God will have no mercy for such fellows, and restrain thyself, Turk, lest thou smash thy head. I send thee five thalers, though I am here in misery and know not what to do, and the household is falling away. I embrace thee, dearest Bartek.

MAGDA.

The teachings contained in this letter made small impression on Bartek. " Women don't know service," thought he to himself, " but are meddlesome." And he fought on in old fashion. He distinguished himself in almost every battle, so that at last eyes of higher rank still than those of Steinmetz fell on him. At last, when the Poznan regiments, wellnigh annihilated, were sent to the interior of Germany, he at the advice of the under-officer sent in a petition and remained. In consequence of this he was outside Paris.

His letters were full of contempt now for the French. " In every battle they tear away from one like hares," wrote he to Magda. And he wrote the truth ! But the siege did not suit his taste greatly. He had to lie in the trenches whole days before Paris, and listen to the thunder of artillery, often to make breastworks and be drenched. Besides, he was sorry for his former regiment. In the one to which he was transferred now as a volunteer he was surrounded

for the greater part by Germans.   Of German
he knew a little, for he had learned some at the
mill, but poorly.   Now he began to talk freely.
Still they called him in the regiment, *Ein
polnischer Ochs*, and only his strong back and
terrible fists saved him from their biting jests.
Still, after a number of battles he acquired the
respect of these new comrades, and began to
grow used to them slowly.   At last he was
looked on as one of them, he had covered the
regiment with glory to such a degree.   Bartek
would have held it an insult at all times to be
called a German (Niemets) but in distinction
to the French he called himself " ein Deutscher."
It seemed to him that that was something
altogether different; and, besides, he did not
wish to appear worse than others.   There was an
event, however, which would have given him
much to think over, had thinking been easier for
his heroic mind.   On a time some men of his
regiment were sent against Volunteer-riflemen,
Franc-tireurs.   They made an ambush, and the

riflemen fell into it. But this time Bartek did not see the red caps flying at the first shots, for the detachment was composed of old soldiers, the remnant of some regiments in a foreign legion. When surrounded, they defended themselves desperately, and at last rushed forward to open with the bayonet a way through the encircling ring of Prussian soldiers. They fought with such fury that some of them broke through. Above all, they did not let themselves be taken alive, knowing the fate which awaited volunteers after capture. Therefore the company in which Bartek served took only two prisoners. In the evening these two men were placed in a room in the forester's house. They were to be shot next morning. Bartek was stationed as guard over the bound prisoners in a room which had a broken window.

One of the prisoners was a man not young, with iron-gray hair and a face indifferent to everything. The other seemed twenty and a few years; his bright mustaches were barely visible; he was more like a woman in the face than a man.

"Yes, here is the end," said the young man, after a while; "a bullet in the forehead, and all is over."

Bartek quivered so that the musket rattled in his hand. The young man spoke Polish.

"It is all one to me," said the other, with unwilling voice, — "as God lives, all one. I have struggled so long that I have enough."

Bartek's heart beat under his uniform more quickly every moment.

"Listen," continued the older; "there is no help. If thou art afraid, think of something else, or lie down to sleep. Life is wretched! As God is dear to me, it is all one."

"I am sorry for my mother," answered the younger one, gloomily.

And wishing evidently to overcome his emotion or to deceive himself, he began to whistle.

Suddenly he stopped, and cried out in deep despair, —

"May the thunderbolt strike me ! I did not even take farewell."

"Thou didst run away from home?"

"I did. I thought: They will beat the Germans, it will be better for the people of Poznan."

"And I thought so too ; but now — "

The old man waved his hand, and finished by saying something in a low voice ; but the sound of the wind drowned his words. The night was cold. Fine rain swept forward in waves from time to time ; the neighboring forest was black as a mourning robe. In the room the wind whistled in the corners, and howled in the chimney like a dog. The lamp, placed high above the window so the wind might not quench it, cast abundant but flickering light on the room. Bartek, who stood under the lamp by the window, was buried in darkness.

And perhaps it was better that the prisoners did not see his face. Wonderful things were happening to the man. At first astonishment took possession of him; he stared at the prisoners, and tried to understand what they were saying. They had come to beat the Germans so that it might go better with the Poznan people; and he had beaten the French so that it might go better with the Poznan people! And those two men will be shot in the morning. What does this mean? What is he, poor fellow, to think of this? And if he were to speak to them, — if he were to tell them that he is of their people, that he is sorry for them? Something seized him all at once by the throat. And what will he tell them, — that he will save them? Then he will be shot! Hei to the rescue! What is happening to him? Pity is so throttling him that he cannot stand in one place.

A certain terrible sadness settles on him from afar, from some place, from Pognembin.

Pity, a strange guest in a soldier's heart, is crying to him: "Bartek, rescue thy own people; these are thine own." And the heart is tearing itself away to his cottage, to Magda, to Pognembin, and tearing itself away in such wise as never before. He has had enough of that France, of that war, and of battles. Every moment he hears a voice more distinctly: "Bartek, save thine own people!" May the earth swallow this war! Through the broken window the forest is black, and it roars like the pines in Pognembin; and in that roar something is crying again: "Bartek, save thine own people!"

What is he to do, — flee with them to the forest, or what? All that Prussian discipline had ever been able to drive into him trembled straightway at that thought. "In the name of the Father and the Son," — this was to defend himself from temptation. He, a soldier, to desert? Never!

Meanwhile the forest roars ever louder.

and the wind whistles more and more mournfully.

The older prisoner speaks suddenly, —

" But that wind is as if in autumn at home."

" Spare me !" said the younger, in a broken voice.

But after a while he repeated a number of times, —

" At home, at home, at home ! O God ! O God !"

A deep sigh was mingled with the whistling, and the prisoners were lying in silence again. Fever began to shake Bartek.

It is worst of all when a man cannot tell what is the matter with him. Bartek had stolen nothing, and it seemed to him as if he had stolen, and as if he feared that they would seize him. Nothing was threatening him, and still he was terribly afraid of something. See, his legs are trembling under him ; his musket weighs him down fearfully, and something is choking him as if it were some great suppressed wailing. Is it for Magda, or for Pognembin? He is sorry for both prisoners, but so sorry for the younger one that he knows not what to do.

At times it seems to Bartek that he is sleeping. Meanwhile the uproar outside is increasing still further. In the whistling of the wind wonderful cries and voices are growing louder.

All at once every hair on Bartek's head stands under his helmet.

See! out there somewhere in the dark, dripping depths of the forest it seems to him that some one is groaning and repeating: "At home, at home, at home!"

Bartek shudders, and strikes the but of his musket on the floor to wake himself. In fact, he returns to consciousness. He looks around; the prisoners are lying in the corner, the lamp is glittering, the wind is howling, everything is in order.

The light is falling now thickly on the face

of the younger prisoner. He has the face of a child or a maiden. But his eyes are closed. There is straw under his head, and he looks as if dead already.

Since Bartek is Bartek never has sadness so dived into him. Something is squeezing him tightly by the throat, a weeping is going out of his breast. Meanwhile the older prisoner turns on his side with difficulty, and says, —

"Good-night, Vladek."

Silence follows. An hour passes. Something really painful has happened to Bartek. The wind is playing like the organs in Pognembin. The prisoners are lying in quiet. Suddenly the younger raises himself with an effort, and calls, —

"Karol!"

"What?"

"Art sleeping?"

"No."

"Listen. I'm afraid; say what may please thee, but I will pray."

" Pray, then."

" Our Father, who art in Heaven, hallowed be Thy name. Thy kingdom come — "

Sobbing interrupted the voice of the young prisoner suddenly; still the broken voice was audible yet, —

" Thy — will — be done — "

" O Jesus ! " howled something in the breast of Bartek, " O Jesus ! "

No, he will endure no longer ! Another moment, and he will cry, " I too am a Pole ! " Then, through the window to the forest, let happen what may !

Suddenly from the direction of the entrance are heard measured steps. That is the patrol, and with him the under-officer. They are changing guards.

On the morrow Bartek was drunk from the morning; the following day also.

.   .   .   .

But on subsequent days new expeditions came, skirmishes, marches, and it is pleasant

for me to relate that our hero returned to
his balance. After that night, however, there
remained with him a little fondness for the
bottle, in which may be found always some
savor and ofttimes forgetfulness. For the rest
he grew still more unsparing in battle; victory
followed his footsteps.

VI.

AGAIN some months passed. The spring
was well advanced. In Pognembin the
cherry-trees had blossomed in the garden, and
were covered with leaves; the fields were green
with a thick fleece. On a certain time Magda
was sitting outside the cottage and preparing for
dinner shrunken sprouted potatoes, fitter food
for cattle than for men. But they were before the new ones. Want had begun to look
in a little at Pognembin. This might be
known, too, from the face of Magda, which

was darkened and full of anxiety. Perhaps, also, to drive away this anxiety the woman, closing her eyes, was singing in a thin, strained voice, —

"Oi, oi, my Yasyenko is at the war! oi! he writes
　　to me,
　Oi! I write to him, oi! for I am his wife."

The sparrows on the cherry-trees were twittering as if they wished to drown her voice; she while singing was looking in thoughtfulness now on the dog sleeping in the sun, now on the road around the cottage, now on the path stretching from the road through the garden and the fields. Perhaps Magda was looking on the path for the reason that it reached across to the station; and God granted that she did not look that day in vain. In the distance appeared a certain form, and the woman shaded her eyes with her hand, but she could not distinguish, for the rays dazzled her; but Lysek the dog woke up, raised his head, barked a little, began to

15

smell, and to incline his head to one side and then to the other. At the same time there came to Magda's ears the uncertain words of a song. Lysek sprang away at once, and ran with all his speed to the man drawing near. Then Magda grew a little pale.

"Bartek, is n't it Bartek?"

She stood up quickly, so that the dish with the potatoes rolled on the ground. Now there was no doubt. Lysek sprang to the breast of the newly-arrived. The woman rushed forward, crying with all her strength and with joy, —

"Bartek! Bartek!"

"Magda! it is I!" cried Bartek, putting his palm to his lips and hurrying his steps.

He opened the gate, missed the bolt, staggered, almost fell, and they dropped into each other's arms.

The woman began to talk quickly.

"But I thought thou wouldst never come back. I thought to myself: 'They have killed him!' How art thou? Come into the cottage. Franek is at school. The German beats the children. The boy is well, but he has staring eyes like thee. Oh, it was time for thee to come, for there is no help, — misery, I say, misery. The poor cottage is rotting down. How art thou? Oh, Bartek, Bartek! That I should look on thee again! What trouble I had here with the hay! The Chermyenitskis helped me, but O my God! — And art thou all well? But I am glad to see thee, glad! God guarded thee. Come in. Oh, for God's sake! is this Bartek, or not Bartek? But what is the matter with thee? Help!"

Magda now noticed for the first time a long scar stretching over Bartek's face, across the left temple and cheek to his beard.

"That's nothing. A cuirassier touched me there, but I paid him. I have been in the hospital."

"O Jesus!"

"Ei, nothing."

"Thou art as thin as death."

"Ruhig (be quiet) !" answered Bartek.

He was swarthy and wounded, a real victor. Withal he was tottering on his feet.

"Art thou drunk?"

"I am weak yet."

He was weak, it is true, but drunk also; exhausted as he was, one measure of *vodka* was enough. Bartek, however, had drunk at the station something like four. But he had the spirit and bearing of a real victor. Such a mien he had never had before.

"Ruhig!" repeated he. "We have finished the *krieg* (war). Now I am a lord, dost understand? Seest this?" Here he pointed to the crosses and medals. "Knowst who I am? He? Links, rechts. Heu, S'troh! Halt! (left, right, hay, straw !) "

He thundered out the last halt! with such a piercing voice that the woman sprang back a number of steps.

"Hast gone mad?"

"How art thou, Magda? When I say to thee,

'How art thou?' that means 'How art thou?'
And knowst French, foolish woman? *musyu,
musyu!* who *musyu?* I *musyu!* knowst?"

"Man, what is the matter with thee?"

"What's that to thee? *Was* (what)? *Done
diner* (donnez diner, — give dinner). Dost
understand?"

On Magda's forehead a storm began to
collect.

"In what language art thou bellowing?
What, knowst thou not Polish? Ha, thou
chestnut, I was right·to say! What have they
made of thee?"

"Give me something to eat!"

"March into the cottage."

Every command made an impression on
Bartek which he could in no way resist. When
he heard then "march" he straightened himself, stretched his arms down along his hips,
and making a half turn marched in the indi-
cated direction. On the threshold he recovered, and began to look at Magda with
astonishment.

"Well, what's the matter, Magda, what's the matter?"

"Forward, march!"

He entered the cottage, but fell at the threshold. The *vodka* began then indeed to go to his head; he fell to singing and looking around the cottage for Franek. He even said, "Morgen, Kerl!" though Franek was not there. Then he laughed, made one long step and two very short ones, shouted hurrah, and stretched his whole length on the floor.

In the evening he woke up sober, refreshed, greeted Franek, and taking some tens of *pfennigs* from Magda, he made a triumphant campaign to the drinking-shop. The fame of his deeds had already preceded him in Pognembin, where some soldiers of the other companies of that same regiment, having returned earlier, told of his prowess at Gravelotte and Sedan. At present, when the news went out that the victor was in the shop, all his old comrades hurried to see him.

Our Bartek sits there at the table. No one recognizes him. He who had been so submissive in old times beats the table with his fist now, swells up like a gobbler, and gobbles like a gobbler.

"Do ye remember, boys, how I warmed up the Frenchmen, and what Steinmetz said?"

"Why should n't we remember?"

"People spoke in favor of the French, frightened us with them; but that is a weak people. *Was* (what)! They are salad. They ride like hares and run like hares, and they don't drink beer, only wine."

"Is that true?"

"When we burned a village they folded their hands and cried out *pitié, pitié!* which seems to mean that they will give drink, but in that tongue it means to spare them. But we paid no attention."

"Can any one understand what they chatter?" asked a young fellow.

"Thou couldst not, for thou art stupid, but

I can. *Done dipen* (give bread), — dost understand?"

"What is that?"

"But have ye seen Paris? There were battles there one after another; but we won them all. They have no good leaders. People say that too, and the officers are fools, and the generals are fools."

Matsyei Kyerz, an old, wise peasant in Pognembin, began to shake his head. "Oi, the Germans have conquered in a terrible war; they have conquered, and we have helped them. But what will come of that to us God alone knows."

Bartek stared at him.   "What do you say?"

"The Germans before this would pay no regard to us, and now they have stuck up their noses as if even God were not above them. And they will insult us more than ever, for they are doing so already."

"That is not true!" said Bartek.

In Pognembin, old Kyerz had such weight that the whole village thought according to his head, and it was insolence to contradict him ; but Bartek was now a victor, himself an authority. Still they looked on him with astonishment, and even with a certain indignation.

"What ! wilt thou dispute with Matsyei? What meanest thou?"

"What is Matsyei to me ! I have spoken with men who are not the like of him. Do ye understand? Have I not spoken with Steinmetz? *Was !* But whatever Matsyei invents is bosh. Now it will be better for us."

Matsyei looked awhile at the victor.

"Oi, but thou art stupid !" said he.

Bartek struck the table with his fist till all the goblets and mugs rattled :

"Still der Kerl da ! Heu, Stroh ! (shut up, fellow, there ! hay, straw !) "

"Be quiet; don't make an uproar. Put the question, thou fool, to some his grace, some lord, and thou wilt find out."

"Was his grace at the war, or was his lordship there? But I was at the war. Don't believe

him, boys; now they will begin to respect us.
Who won the battle? We won it; I won it.
Now whatever I ask for they will give; if I
wanted to be an heir in France I should be one.
The Government knows well who beat the French
best; but our regiments were the best; thus it
was written in the orders. Now the Poles are on
top, do ye understand?"

Kyerz waved his hand, rose, and went out.
Bartek had won the victory on the field of politics also. The young fellows who remained
gazed at him now as at a rainbow.

"But whatever I might ask for they would
give. If it had not been for me then! Old
Kyerz is a fool, do ye understand? The Government commands to fight, then fight! Who will
make light of me, — a German? But what is
this?"

Here he pointed to his crosses and medals
again.

"But for whom did I beat the French, — not
for the Germans. was it? I am now better than

a German, for no German has so many of these. Give us beer! I talked with Steinmetz, and I talked with Podbielski. Give beer!"

Gradually they prepared for a drinking bout. Bartek began to sing, —

> "Drink, drink, drink!
> While in my purse
> A thaler clinks."

Suddenly he drew out of his pocket a handful of *pfennigs*.

"Take these, — I am a lord now, — do ye not want them? Oh, not this kind of money did we get in France, but it is gone. Little that we did n't burn up and kill. God knows whom not — *Frantsirerov* (Franc-tireurs)."

The humor of men in drink changes very suddenly. Unexpectedly Bartek gathered the money from the table and began to cry piteously:

"God be merciful to my sinful soul!"

Then he placed his elbows on the table, hid his face in his paws, and was silent.

"What's the matter with thee?" asked some of the tipsy ones.

"How am I to blame?" muttered Bartek, gloomily. "They came themselves. I was sorry for them, for they were both of my people. O God, be merciful! One of them was as ruddy as the dawn then, but next morning he was pale as a kerchief, and while still alive they were covered with earth. — Vodka!"

A moment of gloomy silence followed. The men looked at one another in astonishment.

"What is he saying?" asked some one.

"He is saying something to his conscience."

"Without war a man drinks," muttered Bartek.

He drank *vodka* once, and a second time. He sat awhile in silence, then spat; and good humor returned to him suddenly.

"But have ye talked with Steinmetz? I have talked with him. Hurrah! Drink! Who will pay? I!"

"Thou wilt pay, drunkard, thou!" called the voice of Magda; "but I 'll pay thee, never fear."

Bartek looked at the newly-arrived woman with glassy eyes.

"But hast thou talked with Steinmetz? Who art thou?"

Magda instead of answering him turned to his sensitive audience and began to lament.

"Oh, people, people, ye see my shame and my suffering. He came home. I rejoiced as at something good; but he came drunk, and forgot God, forgot Polish. He lay down to sleep, grew sober; and now he is drinking again, and pays with my sweat. Where didst thou get that money; was that not my toil, my blood-sweat? Oh, people, people, he is not a Catholic any longer, not a man. He is a raging German, chatters German, lies in wait to do evil; he is a turn-coat, he is —"

Here the woman was covered with tears; then she raised her voice an octave higher:

" He was stupid but good. Now what have they made of him? I waited for thee evenings, I waited for thee mornings, and waited till thou didst come home. From no place consolation, from no place mercy. God of might! God of patience! Mayst thou turn into German altogether!"

She finished the last words so sorrowfully that she was almost whining. But Bartek in answer said, —

" Be quiet, or I will rush at thee!"

" Strike, cut off my head, cut it off right away, kill, murder!" called the woman, stubbornly, and stretching out her neck, turned to the men:

" And you men look at him doing it."

But the men began to go out. Soon the shop was empty; only Bartek remained, and the woman with her neck stretched out.

" Why stretch out thy neck like a goose? Go to the cottage," muttered Bartek.

" Cut it off!" repeated Magda.

" But I will not cut it off," answered Bartek, and put his hands in his pockets.

Here the shopkeeper, wishing to put an end to the incident, quenched the only candle. There was darkness and silence. After a time in the darkness was heard the whining voice of Magda, —

" Cut off my head."

" I will not cut it off," answered the triumphant voice of Bartek.

By the light of the moon were to be seen two forms going from the shop toward the cottages ; one of them in advance, was lamenting audibly. That was Magda. After her, with drooping head, went submissively enough the victor of Gravelotte and Sedan.

VII.

BARTEK came home, but so weak that he could not work for a number of days. This was a great misfortune for the whole house-keeping, which had urgent need of a man's hand. Magda did the best she could, — worked from morning till night. Her neighbors the Chemyer-nitskis helped her according to their power ; but all that was not enough, and the place was in-clining somewhat toward ruin. She had gone in debt too to the colonist Just, a German, who in his time had bought from the lord some acres of poor land, and had now the best place in the village, and ready money, which he lent at rather high interest. He lent first of all to Pan Yarzynski, whose name Yarzynski was gleaming in the "Golden Book," but who on that account had to maintain the splendor of

his house in befitting style; but Just lent also
to peasants. Magda owed him, for about half a
year, a few tens of thalers, some of which she
expended on the land, and some she sent to
Bartek. That however was nothing. God had
given a good harvest, and from the coming fruits
the debt might be paid if there were only hands
to labor. Unfortunately Bartek could not work.
Magda was not greatly willing to believe this,
and went to the priest to take counsel as to how
she might rouse the man; but he was in fact unable to work. Breath failed him when he labored
a little, and his back ached. He sat whole days
therefore before the cottage, and smoked a porcelain pipe on which was a portrait of Bismarck,
in a white uniform and a cuirassier's helmet.
Bartek looked on the world with the wearied
sleepy eye of a man out of whose bones toil has
not gone yet. At the same time he pondered a
little over the war, a little over victories, over
Magda, a little over everything, a little over
nothing.

Once as he was sitting thus he heard from a distance the crying of Franek.

Franek was coming from school, and bellowing to be heard all over the place. Bartek took the pipe from his mouth.

" Well, Franek, what is the matter? "

" But what is that to thee? " said Franek, sobbing.

" Why bellow? "

" Why should n't I bellow when I got a slap on the face? "

" Who gave thee a slap on the face? "

" Who, unless Pan Boege ! "

Pan Boege performed the duties of teacher in Pognembin.

" And what right has he to beat thee on the face? "

" He has, for he beat me."

Magda, who was digging in the garden, came in through the fence, and with a spade in her hand came up to the boy.

" What hast thou done? " asked she.

"Nothing. But Boege called me a Polish pig, slapped me on the face, and said that now as they had beaten the French they would stamp on us, for they are stronger; but I did nothing to him. Only he asked who was the greatest person in the world, and I said 'The Holy Father.' Pan Boege slapped me on the face. I began to cry, and he called me a Polish pig, and said that now as they had beaten the French — "

Franek began to repeat what he had said before : "and he said and I said." At last Magda covered his face with her hand, and turning to Bartek, cried out, —

"Dost hear, dost hear? Go thou and beat the French, and then let the German beat thy child as he would the dog there ! Go thou ! fight ! Let a Schwab beat thy child ! Now thou hast a reward, thou lout."

Here Magda, moved by her own words, began to cry too, as well as Franek. Bartek stared, opened his mouth, and was amazed so much that he could not speak, and above all could not understand what had happened. How is that? But his victories? He sat awhile longer in silence. On a sudden something gleamed in his eyes, blood rushed to his face. Amazement, as well as terror, frequently passes into rage with simple people. Bartek sprang up quickly, and rushed forth with set teeth.

"I'll talk to him!" and he went on. It was not far. The school was right there beyond the church. Pan Boege was standing at that moment before his door, surrounded by a crowd of pigs, among which he was throwing bits of bread. He was a large man about fifty years old, strong yet as an oak. He was not over thick; but he had a very full face, and in his face were great fish eyes with an expression of boldness and energy. Bartek came up very near him.

"Why dost thou, German, beat my child? *Was!*" inquired he.

Pan Boege stepped back a few yards, measured him with his eyes without a shadow of fear, and said phlegmatically: "Be off!"

"Why didst thou beat my child?" repeated Bartek.

"I 'll beat thee too, Polish trash! Now we 'll show thee who is lord here. Go to the devil! Go with complaint to the court! Be off!"

Bartek, seizing the teacher by the shoulders, began to shake him powerfully, crying with hoarse voice:

"Knowest who I am? Knowest who pounded the French? Knowest who talked with Steinmetz? Why beat my child, Schwab, lout?"

The fish eyes of Pan Boege were coming out of his head not less than Bartek's; but he was a strong man, and determined to free himself from the aggressor with one blow.

This blow was a powerful slap on the face of the victor of Gravelotte and Sedan. Thereupon Bartek lost self-control. Boege's head was shaken with two heavy movements reminding one of the movement of a pendulum, with this difference, — that the shaking was astonishingly quick. In Bartek the terrible crusher of the Tur-

kos and Zouaves was aroused anew.   In vain did
the twelve-year old Oscar, son of Boege, a boy
strong like his father, hasten to help him.   A
struggle began, short and terrible, in which the
son fell to the ground and the father felt himself
raised in the air.   Bartek, with arms stretched
aloft, bore him, whither he knew not himself.
Unfortunately there stood near the house a barrel of swill industriously poured in for the pigs
by Pani Boege ; and behold there was a plash in
the barrel, and in a moment were seen the legs
of Boege sticking out of it and kicking violently.
Boege's wife rushed out of the house :

"Help, rescue ! "

The woman with presence of mind turned
the barrel over in a moment and spilled out her
husband together with the swill.   The German
colonists hastened from the houses near by to
help their neighbor.

A number of Germans hurled themselves on
Bartek and began to belabor him, some with
clubs, others with fists.   A general chaos arose,

in which it was difficult to distinguish Bartek from his enemies. A number of bodies were entangled in one mass moving convulsively. But suddenly from out the mass of strugglers rushed forth Bartek, wild, shooting off with all power toward the fence.

The Germans sprang after him; but at the same moment a crash in the fence was heard, and that instant a strong pole was brandished in the iron paws of Bartek. He turned, foaming at the mouth, raging; he raised his hands with the club in the air; all fled. Bartek followed them. Happily he overtook no man. Presently he came to himself, and began to retreat toward his cottage. Ah, had he the French before him history would have immortalized that retreat!

It was as follows: The attackers, to the number of twelve men, rallied and pressed again on Bartek. He retreated slowly, like a wild boar pressed by dogs. At times he turned and halted; then the pursuers restrained themselves. The club had won their perfect respect.

But they threw stones. One of these stones wounded Bartek in the forehead. Blood covered his eyes. He felt that he was growing weak. He staggered once and a second time, dropped the club, and fell.

" Hurrah ! " cried the colonists.

But before they came up Bartek had risen ; that restrained them. The wounded wolf might be dangerous yet. Moreover the first cottages were not far, and from a distance were to be seen a number of Polish peasants running with all speed to the scene of combat. The colonists withdrew to their houses.

" What has happened ? " asked those who ran up.

" Dressing the Germans," said Bartek, and he fainted.

VIII.

THE affair assumed threatening proportions. The German papers contained rousing articles about the persecutions which peaceable Germans were suffering from the barbarous and ignorant mass excited by anti-aristocratic agitation and religious fanaticism. Boege became a hero. He, the teacher mild and gentle, spreading enlightenment along the distant borders of the State ; he, the true missionary of culture among barbarians, was the first to fall a victim to their fury. It was fortunate that behind him were a hundred millions of Germans who will not permit, etc. —

Bartek knew not what a storm was gathering above his head ; but he was of good heart, he felt sure of winning before the court. Boege had beaten his child and had struck him first, and afterward so many attacked him. He had to defend himself of course. Besides, they opened his head with a stone. Whose head? The head of the man distinguished in the orders of the day, of the man who had "gained" the battle of Gravelotte, who had talked with Steinmetz himself, and who had so many crosses. He could not in truth understand how the Germans could know all this and still work such injustice on him; nor how Boege could promise the men of Pognembin that the Germans would trample them now because they, the men of Pognembin, had beaten the French so valiantly whenever opportunity offered. But as to himself he was certain that the court and the Government would take his part. They at least will know who he is, what he has done in the war; even if no one else does, Steinmetz will take his part. Besides, Bartek has grown poor through the war; his cottage is mortgaged. They will not deny him justice.

Meanwhile the police come to Pognembin for Bartek. They expected to find terrible resistance, for they came with five loaded muskets. They were mistaken. Bartek did not think of resistance. They ordered him to sit in the wagon. He sat in it. Magda was in despair, only she repeated persistently, —

"Oh, there was need of thy fighting the French so! thou hast got it now, poor man, — thou hast got it!"

"Be quiet, foolish woman," said Bartek; and he smiled along the road gladly enough at passers-by.

"I will show them who did the injustice!" cried he from the wagon.

And with his crosses on his breast he went like a conqueror to the court. In fact, the court showed itself gracious toward him; extenuating circumstances were found. Bartek was condemned to only three months' imprisonment; besides this, he was condemned to pay one hundred and fifty marks as a recompense to the family of Boege and to other corporeally injured colonists.

"The criminal however," said the "Posener Zeitung" in the report of the case, "when the sentence was read to him, did not exhibit the least repentance, but burst out with such rude words, and began to reproach the State so shamefully with his pretended services, that there is reason to wonder why the attorney present did not begin a new suit against him for his insults to the court and to the German race."

Meanwhile Bartek in prison meditated calmly over his deeds of Gravelotte, Sedan, and Paris. We should be unjust, however, were we to say that Boege's act called forth no public comment. It did, it did. On a certain rainy morning some Polish member in the German Parliament showed very eloquently how the treatment of Poles in Poznan had changed; and that for the bravery of the Poznan regiments, and the losses incurred by them during the war, it would be proper to think more of the rights of people in the province of Poznan;

finally, how Pan Boege of Pognembin had abused his position of teacher by beating Polish children, calling them Polish swine, and promising that after such a war an intrusive element would trample under foot the original inhabitants.

While the member was speaking, the rain was falling; and since on such a day drowsiness seizes men, the Conservatives were yawning; the Centre — for the *Kultur Kampf* had not begun yet — was yawning.

At last, in answer to the Polish complaint, the House returned to the order of the day.

Meanwhile Bartek was sitting in prison, or rather lying in the prison hospital, for from the blow of the stone the wound he had received in the war opened. When he had not the fever, he was thinking like that turkey gobbler which died from thought. Bartek did not die however; still he thought out nothing. But sometimes in moments which science calls *lucid intervals*, it came to his head that perhaps he had pounded the French without need.

On Magda came grievous times. The fine
had to be paid; there was no place in which
to get the money. The priest of Pognembin
wanted to help her; but it turned out that in
his treasury there were not forty whole marks.
The parish of Pognembin was a poor one;
besides, the old man never knew how his
money was expended. Pan Yarzynski was not
at home; people said that he had gone to
court some wealthy young lady in the Kingdom.
Magda knew not what to do. An extension
of the term was not to be thought of. What
then? To sell the horse or a cow? and it was
just before harvest, — the most difficult period.
Grain-cutting was at hand. The woman needed
money, and had spent all her store of it. She
wrung her hands in despair; she sent a number
of petitions to the court, asking for extension,
recounting Bartek's services. She did not get
even an answer. The term was approaching,
and with it an execution. She prayed and
prayed, thinking bitterly of times before the

war when they were rich, and when Bartek was earning money in winter at the mill. She went to her friends to borrow money; but they had none. The war had paid all with marks of distinction. To Just she did not dare to go, for she was already in debt to him, and had not paid even the interest. But Just himself came to her unexpectedly.

On a certain afternoon she was sitting on the threshold of her cottage doing nothing, for the strength had gone out of her from despair. She was looking out at the golden flies chasing through the air, and she thought how happy are those insects, playing for themselves, and not crying. At times she sighed heavily, or from her pale lips came the quiet exclamation, " O God ! O God ! " All at once before the gate appeared the hanging nose of Just, under which was a hanging pipe. Just called out, —

" Morgen ! "

" How is your health, Pan Just ? "

" But my money ? "

"Oh, my dear, golden Pan Just, be patient! What shall I, poor woman, do? They have taken my man; I must pay the fine for him. I don't know what to do. Better die than suffer from day to day as I suffer. Wait a little, my golden Pan Just."

She burst into tears, and, bending down, kissed submissively the thick red hand of Pan Just.

"Pan Yarzynski will come; I will get money from him, and pay you."

"But how will you pay the fine?"

"How do I know unless I sell a cow?"

"Well, I will lend you more money."

"May the Lord God reward you, my golden Pan. Although a Lutheran, you are a good man; I say indeed that if other Germans were like you, a man might bless them."

"But I will not give it without interest."

"I know, I know."

"Then you write me one note for all you owe."

"I will, golden Pan; God reward you even for that!"

"I will be in town, and we will draw up the paper."

He went to town, and had the paper drawn up; but Magda went first to take counsel with the priest. But what counsel was there to be taken? The priest said that the term was too short, that the interest was too high, and grieved greatly that Pan Yarzynski was not at home; for if he had been at home, he might help. But Magda could not wait till the court sold her effects, and was forced to accept Just's conditions.

She went in debt three hundred marks; that is, twice as much as the "fine," for she needed some money in the house to carry on affairs. Bartek, who had to confirm the act with his own signature, to give it validity, signed it. Magda for that purpose went to him in prison. The victor was greatly weighed down, crushed, and sick. He wrote another complaint, and set

17

forth his wrongs ; but his complaint was not received. The articles in the " Posener Zeitung "
had roused opinions in Government circles
with too great unfriendliness toward him.
Were the authorities to refuse protection to that
peaceable German population, " which in the
last war had given so many proofs of its love
for the country and for enlightenment " ? Justly,
therefore, was Bartek's complaint rejected.
But be not surprised if that crushed him
completely.

" We shall be lost altogether," said he, to his
wife.

" Altogether," repeated she.

Bartek began to think over something powerfully.

" I am terribly wronged," said he.

" Boege is tormenting the boy," said Magda.
" I went to entreat him ; he abused me more.
' Oi !' said he, ' the Germans are on top now
in Poznan. They are afraid of nobody
now.' "

"It is sure that they are stronger," said Bartek, gloomily.

"I'm a simple woman; but I say this, that God is stronger."

"In Him is our refuge," added Bartek.

Both were silent awhile; then they asked again, —

"Well, and what of Just?"

"May the highest God give us harvest! perhaps we may pay him some way. Perhaps, too, Pan Yarzynski will help us, though he himself is in debt to the Germans. Even before the war it was said that he must sell Pognembin. Perhaps he will marry a rich woman."

"But will he come soon?"

"Who knows? They say at the mansion that he'll come soon with his wife. The Germans will crowd him when he comes. Those Germans are crawling in everywhere like worms. Wherever thy eyes look, wherever thou canst turn, in the village or the town,

— Germans ! It must be in punishment for our sins. And rescue from no side ! "

"Maybe thou canst do something ; thou art a wise woman."

"What can I do, what? Did I borrow money from Just of my own will? In good right, the cottage in which we are, and the land too, is his now. Just is a better German than others ; but he has his own good in mind, and not ours. He will not spare us, as he has not spared others. Am I such a fool as not to know why he offers me money? But what is to be done ! what is to be done ! " said Magda, wringing her hands ; "tell, tell, if thou art wise. Thou wert able to beat the French ; but what wilt thou do when there is no roof over thy head, nor a spoonful of food for thy mouth ? "

The victor of Gravelotte seized his head, —

"O Jesus ! O Jesus ! "

Magda had a good heart ; Bartek's pain moved her : she said at once. —

"Be quiet, poor fellow, be quiet; do not seize thy head, for it is not healed yet. If God gives a harvest! The rye is so beautiful that one would like to kiss the land; and the wheat is beautiful. The land is not a German, — it will not wrong thee. Even though without thy war the field was worked stupidly, still there is such a growth that — "

Honest Magda laughed through her tears, —

"The land is not a German," repeated she again.

"Magda," said Bartek, looking at her with his staring eyes, "Magda ! "

"What?"

"But thou art — as — "

Bartek felt for her great thankfulness; but he knew not how to express it.

IX.

MAGDA was, indeed, worth as much as ten women worse than herself. She held her Bartek rather strictly; but she was really attached to him. In moments of excitement, as, for instance, that time in the shop, she told him to his eyes that he was a fool; but in general she wished people to think otherwise. "My Bartek seems dull, but he is cunning," said she, frequently. Meanwhile Bartek was as cunning as his own horse; and without Magda he would not have been able to get on either in housekeeping or aught else. Now everything was on her honest head; and she began to hurry about, to run, to entreat, so that she found rescue at last. A week after her first visit to the prison hospital, she rushed in again to Bartek, panting, happy, radiant.

" How art thou, Bartek, thou Chestnut?"
cried she with joy. "Pan Yarzynski has come,
— knowest thou? He got married in the Kingdom; the young lady is a berry. And he got
all kinds of riches with her."

" Well, but what of that?" inquired Bartek.

" Be quiet, stupid fellow!" answered Magda.
" I went to bow down to the Pani; I look — she
comes out to me like some queen, so young, as
beautiful as the dawn."

Magda raised her apron, and began to wipe
her face. After a while she spoke again, with a
broken voice, —

" She wore a robe blue as a star-thistle. I fell
at her feet, and she gave me her hand; I kissed
it; and her hands are sweet and small as a
child's hands. She is like a saint in a picture;
and she is good, and understands the sufferings
of people. I began to entreat her to save us,
that God might reward her! And she said,
' What is in my power I will do.' And she has
a dear voice; so that when she speaks a sweet-

ness takes hold of thee. When I told how
unhappy people were in Pognembin, she said,
'Ai, not only in Pognembin!' and when I
broke out crying, she cried as well, till her husband came in, and saw that she was crying.
Then he took her, and kissed her on the mouth
and on the eyes. Lords are not like peasants!
Then she said to him, 'Do what thou canst for
this woman!' And he answered, 'Everything
in the world according to thy wish.' May the
Mother of God bless her, the golden berry!
bless her with children, with health! 'Ye are
greatly to blame,' said Pan Yarzynski, 'for putting yourselves into German hands; but,' said
he, 'I will save you, and give you the money
for Just.'"

Bartek began to scratch his neck.

"But the Germans had him in hand, too."

"What of that? But the lady is rich. Now
they can buy out all the Germans in Pognembin, so he can talk that way. 'The election is
coming,' said he; 'let the people be careful not

to vote for Germans. I will give the money for Just, and tame Boege.' And the lady put her arms around his neck, and he inquired about thee, and said: 'If he is weak I will ask the doctor to write a certificate that he cannot sit out his term at present. If they do not free him entirely, let him stay out his term in winter; but now he is needed for the harvest.' Dost hear? Yesterday, Pan Yarzynski was in the town, and to-day the doctor will come to Pognembin on a visit, for he was asked. He is not a German, and he will write a certificate. In the winter thou 'lt be in prison like a king in his castle; it will be warm for thee there, and they 'll give thee to eat for nothing; and now thou 'lt go home to work, and we 'll pay Just, and maybe Pan Yarzynski will not want any interest. And if we do not pay all in the autumn I 'll speak to the lady. May the Mother of God reward her! Dost hear?"

"She is a good lady; there is nothing to be said against that," said Bartek, quickly.

"Thou wilt fall at her feet, thou 'lt fall; if not I 'll twist thy yellow head off. If God gives a good harvest — Dost see where rescue came from? From the Germans? Did they give thee even one copper for thy stupid work, did they? They gave thee a blow on the head, that 's all. Thou 'lt fall at the lady's feet, I tell thee."

"Why not fall?" answered Bartek, resolutely.

Fate seemed to smile again on the victor. A few days later it was announced to him that for reasons of health he was liberated till winter. But the Landrath commanded Bartek to appear before him. Bartek came with his soul on his shoulder. That man who with bayonet in hand took standards and cannon, began to fear every uniform more than death, — began to bear in his heart a certain dull, unconscious feeling that they were persecuting him, that they could do what they liked with him, that there was above him a certain enormous power, hostile and malevolent, which would grind him if he opposed it. He stood then before the Landrath, as once he had stood before Steinmetz, erect, with his stomach drawn in, his breast pushed forward, without breath in his bosom. There were a number of officers there also; war and military discipline stood as if living before Bartek. The officers looked at him through their gold-rimmed glasses with the pride and contempt which should be shown a common soldier and a Polish peasant by Prussian officers. Bartek held his breath, and the Landrath spoke in a commanding tone. He did not request, he did not persuade; he commanded, he threatened. The member had died in Berlin, a new election was ordered.

"Du polnisches Vieh (Thou Polish beast)! just try to vote for Pan Yarzynski, try!"

The brows of the officers were contracted at that moment in terrible lion wrinkles. One, biting a cigar, repeated after the Landrath, "try," and the breath died in Bartek the victor.   When he heard the desired "Go out !" he made a half turn to the left, went out, and drew breath.

The command was issued to him to vote for Pan Schulberg from Upper Kryvda.   He did not think over the command ; but he breathed, he went to Pognembin, for he could be home for the harvest.   Pan Yarzynski had promised to pay Just.   Bartek went outside the town.   He was surrounded by fields of ripening grain.   One head heavy with the wind strikes another head and rustles with a sound dear to the ear of the peasant.   Bartek was weak yet, but the sun warmed him.   "Hei, how beautiful it is in the world !" thought the broken soldier.   And it is not far now to Pognembin.

X.

THE election! the election! Pani Marya Yarzynski has her head full of it; she thinks not, she speaks not, she dreams not of anything else.

"The lady benefactress is a great politician," says a neighboring noble, kissing like a dragon her small hands; and the "great politician" blushes like a cherry, and answers with a pretty smile, —

"We agitate as far as we are able."

"Pan Yozef will be elected," said the noble, convincingly, and the "great politician" answers, —

"I should like it greatly, though the question is not merely of Yozio, but [here the "great politician" was cooking again the unpolitical lobster] of the common cause."

"A real Bismarck, as I love God!" cries
the noble, and again he kisses the small hand.
Again the two take counsel about the agitation.
The noble takes on himself Lower Kryvda and
Mizerov (Upper Kryvda is lost, for its owner
is Pan Schulberg) and Pani Marya is to occupy
herself beyond all with Pognembin. Her head
was on fire because she was playing such a
rôle. Indeed, she lost no time. Every day
she was to be seen on the high road among
the cottages, her skirt raised with one hand,
her little parasol in the other, and from under
the skirt peeped forth her dainty feet, trotting
around eagerly for great political objects. She
enters the cottages of laboring people, says
on the way, "God give assistance!" She visits
the sick, occupies herself with the people,
helps where she can; she would have done
that without politics, for she has a good heart;
but all the more for politics. What would she
not do for politics? But she does not dare
to confess to her husband that she has an

irresistible desire to go to the village court; she even put together in her head a speech proper to be made there. What a speech! what a speech! In truth she would not really speak it; but if she should speak it, then? When the news came to Pognembin that the authorities had dissolved the court, the "great politician" burst out from anger in her room, tore her handkerchief, and had red eyes all day. In vain did her husband entreat her not to demean herself to that degree. Next morning the agitation was carried on in Pognembin with still greater intensity. Pani Marya did not retreat before anything. In one day she was at a number of cottages, and jeered at the Germans so loudly that her husband had to restrain her. But there is no danger; the people receive her with joy, kiss her hands, and smile at her, for she is so shapely, so rosy, that when she enters a house it grows bright. In turn she came to Bartek's cottage. Lysek the dog would

not let her in, but Magda in her anger gave
him a blow of a club on the head.

"Oh, serene lady, my golden lady, my
beauty, my berry!" cried Magda, nestling up
to her hands.

Bartek, in obedience to command, throws
himself at her feet; little Franek first of
all kisses her hand, then puts his finger in
his mouth, and buries himself wholly in
wonderment.

"I hope," said the young lady, after the
greetings were over, "I hope, my Bartek,
that you will vote for my husband, not for
Pan Schulberg."

"Oh, my dawn!" cried Magda, "who would
vote for Schulberg? May the paralysis strike
him! [Here she kissed the lady's hand.]
Let not the serene lady be angry; but
when a German is mentioned, it is hard to
hold the tongue."

"My husband has told me that he will pay
Just."

"May God bless him!" Here Magda turned to Bartek. "Why stand like a post? He, my lady, is terribly silent."

"You will vote for my husband," asked the lady, "will you not? You are Poles, we are Poles; we will hold together."

"I would twist his head off if he did n't vote," said Magda. "Why stand like a post? He is terribly silent. Stir up!"

Bartek kisses the hand of the lady again; but is silent all the time and gloomy as night. He is thinking of the Landrath.

. . . .

The day of the election is coming, has come. Pan Yarzynski is certain of victory. The nobles have returned from the town; they have already voted, and will wait now in Pognembin for the news which the priest will bring. There will be a dinner after that; in the evening the Yarzynskis will go to Poznan, and then to Berlin. Some villages in the electoral district had voted the day before; the result will be known to-day.

18

The company, however, is in good spirits. The youthful lady is a little disquieted, but full of hope and smiles. She is such a welcoming lady that all say, " Pan Yarzynski has found a real treasure in the Kingdom." That " treasure " cannot indeed sit quietly in one place just now, but is running from guest to guest, and commands each a hundred times to give the assurance that " Yozio will be elected." She is not really ambitious, and not from vanity does she wish to become the wife of a member; but she has imagined in her young head that she and her husband have a real mission to perform. Her heart therefore is beating as quickly as at the moment of her marriage, and joy lights up her pretty face. Making her way deftly through the guests, she approaches her husband, draws him by the sleeve, and whispers into his ear like a child who is nick-naming some one, " Pan Posel (Sir Member)." He smiles, and both are happy beyond expression. Both have a great desire to kiss each other, but that is not

proper before guests. All are looking every
moment through the window, for the cause is
really important. The member who had died
recently was a Pole, and this was the first time
that the Germans had brought out a candidate
in the district. Clearly a victorious war had
given them boldness; but for that reason it was
important to the company assembled in the
mansion of Pognembin that their candidate be
chosen. There was no lack either before the
dinner, of patriotic utterances, which moved
especially the youthful lady, so unaccustomed
to them. At moments she had attacks of fear:
But if some fraud should be committed in counting the votes? But Germans are not alone in
the committee. The older inhabitants explained
then to the lady how the counting of votes is
carried on. She had heard it about a hundred
times, but wishes to hear it again, for the
question is: Are the people of that place to
have a defender in Parliament or an enemy?
That will be decided soon indeed, for on the

road a cloud of dust rises suddenly. "The priest is coming, the priest is coming!" repeat those present. The lady grows pale. On all faces excitement is evident. They are certain of victory; but still the last moment increases the beating of hearts. But that is not the priest; it is the land-steward returning on horseback from the town. Maybe he knows something? He ties the horse to the ring and hurries to the house. The guests, with the lady in front of them, rush out to the porch.

"Have you news? Is our host elected? What? Come here! You know surely? Is the result announced?"

Questions cross each other and fall like rockets. The man throws his cap in the air.

"Our lord is elected."

The lady drops suddenly on the bench and presses her swelling bosom with her hand.

"Vivat! vivat!" cried the neighbors. "Vivat!"

The servants rush out of the kitchen: "Vivat! The Germans are beaten! Long life to the new member and the lady!"

"But the priest?" inquires some one.

"He will be here soon," said the land-steward; "they are still counting the last names."

"Bring in the dinner!" cries the new member.

"Vivat!" repeat others.

All return from the porch to the hall. Congratulations to the lord and the lady are now flowing more calmly; but the lady herself is not able to restrain her joy, and without thinking of spectators throws her arms around her husband's neck. But they do not take that ill of her; nay, emotion seizes all.

"We shall live yet," says a neighbor from Mizerov.

That moment a rattling is heard at the porch; the priest enters the hall, and with him old Kyerz from Pognembin.

"We greet, we greet!" cry the guests. "Well, what was the majority?"

The priest, silent for an instant, casts as it were in the face of the general rejoicing harshly and briefly two words, —

"Schulberg elected!"

A moment of astonishment, a hail-storm of questions hurried and disturbed, to which the priest answers again, —

"Schulberg elected!"

"How? What has happened? In what way? The land-steward said he was not. What has happened?"

At that moment Pan Yarzynski conducted out of the hall poor Pani Marya, who was gnawing her handkerchief to avoid bursting into tears or fainting.

"O misfortune! misfortune!" repeat the guests, seizing themselves by their heads.

At that moment from the direction of the village comes the sound of distant voices as if joyous shouts. That is the Germans of

Pognembin going around joyfully with their victory.

The Yarzynskis return to the hall. It was to be heard how at the door the young man said to the lady, "Il faut faire bonne mine. (We must put a good face on it)." In fact the lady was weeping no longer; she had dry eyes, and was greatly flushed.

"Tell us now how it happened," said the host, calmly.

"How could it not happen, serene lord," said old Kyerz, "when the peasants here in Pognembin voted for Schulberg?"

"Who, — these here? But how was that?"

"They did. I myself saw, and all saw, how Bartek Slovik voted for Schulberg."

"Bartek Slovik?" said the lady.

"Of course. Now the others are railing at him, the man is rolling on the ground; he is weeping, his wife is abusing him. But I saw myself how he voted."

"Such a man should be driven from the village," said a neighbor from Mizerov.

"Well, serene lord," said Kyerz, "others too who were at the war voted that way as well as he. They say that they were commanded."

"Abuse, pure abuse! the election is not valid. Constraint, fraud!" cried various voices.

Not joyful was the dinner of that day in the Pognembin mansion. In the evening the Yarzynskis went away, — but not to Berlin, only to Dresden.

Miserable, cursed, despised, and hated, Bartek sat in his cottage, a stranger even to his own wife, for she had not spoken a word to him the whole day.

.   .   .   .

God gave a bountiful harvest, and in the autumn Pan Just, who had now taken possession of Bartek's place, was glad that he had done a business that was not at all bad.

On a certain day three people were going from Pognembin to the town, a man, a woman, and a boy. The man, greatly bent, was more like some old grandfather than a healthy person. They were going to the town, for in Pognembin they could not find work. The rain was falling; the woman was sobbing terribly in grief for the lost cottage and the whole village, the man was silent. The whole road was empty, neither a wagon nor a man, — only the cross stretched over the wayside, its arms wet from rain. The rain fell more and more densely, and it was growing dark in the world.

Bartek, Magda, and Franek were going to the town; the victor of Gravelotte and Sedan had to serve out his time in prison for the Boege affair.

The Yarzynskis continued to live in Dresden.